Sign up for book announcements and special deals at:

AWBALDWIN.COM

ACCLAIM FOR THE

RELIC SERIES NOVELS

BY AWARD WINNING AUTHOR

A.W. BALDWIN

DESERT GUARDIAN

A moonshining hermit.
A campus bookworm.
A midnight murder.

Can an unlikely duo and a whitewater crew save themselves and an ancient Aztec battlefield from deadly looters?

Ethan's world turns upside-down when he slips off the edge of red-rock cliffs into a world of twisting ravines and coveted artifacts. Saved by a mysterious desert recluse named Relic, Ethan must join a whitewater rafting group and make his way back to civilization. But someone in the gorge is killing to protect their illegal dig for ancient treasures... When Anya, the lead whitewater guide, is attacked, he must divert the killer into the dark canyon night, but his most deadly pursuer is not who he thinks... Ethan struggles to save his new friends, face his own mortality, and unravel the chilling murders. But when they flee the secluded canyon, a lethal hunter is hot on their trail…

Reviews on Amazon say:

"full of suspense…you will be deeply involved from the moment you begin."

"ingenious plot, gorgeous setting, intriguing characters, great read."

"loved the mysterious character *Relic.*"

Five Star Rating from Readers' Favorite:

Desert Guardian is an "engaging action… mystery." The novel has "tough, credible characters"

"A.W. Baldwin's writing is clear, fluid, and very detailed."

RAPTOR CANYON

A moonshining hermit.
A big city lawyer.
A $35 million con job.

What if you discover you've helped your boss hide a murder and defile a pristine canyon? Can a young lawyer and moonshining hermit save rare petroglyphs and monkey-wrench a corrupt land deal in the Utah canyons?

An impromptu murder leads a hermit named Relic to an unlikely set of dinosaur petroglyphs and swindlers using the unique rock art to turn the canyon into a high-end tourist trap. When attorney, Wyatt, and his boss travel to the site to approve the next phase of financing, Wyatt learns the truth about their unorthodox role in the project. A corrupt security chief runs Relic and Wyatt off of the site and the unusual pair must endure each other while fleeing though white-water rapids, remote gorges, and hidden caverns. Faye, who shares covert ties with the treasured site, catalyzes their desperate plan to fight back and to recast the fate of Raptor Canyon.

Grand Master Adventure Writers' Finalist Award 2019

ScreenCraft Cinematic Book Contest Finalist 2019-2020

"A captivating joyride through the mystical southwest canyonlands as a modern day monkey-wrench gang fights for the preservation of the land and their own survival. Relentless danger mixed with dusty adventure makes for a gem of a read."

– Dirk Cussler, #1 New York Times Best-selling Author

"Raptor Canyon will have you holding your breath and your heart at the same time…"

– Peter Greene, award winning author of the *Adventures of Jonathan Moore* series

"Hold onto your hat! A ripping adventure romp set in the twists and turns of Utah's canyon country… Thoroughly entertaining!"

– Jacob P. Avila, *Cave Diver*, Grand Master Adventure Writers' Award Winner

"Raptor Canyon is a ton of fun… the playful dialogue between Wyatt and Relic was a pleasure to read… Highly recommended!"

– Landon Beach, Bestselling author of *The Sail*, Grand Master Adventure Writers' Finalist Award

Five Star Rating from Readers' Favorite:

"A hoot of an adventure novel… most highly recommended."

Onlinebookclub.org four out of four Star Review:

"…captivating, with hair raising experiences that will have your muscles tensed up and your heart pounding… I enthusiastically recommend it to anyone who enjoys mesmerizing, fast-paced novels."

WINGS OVER GHOST CREEK

A moonshining hermit.
A reluctant pilot.
A $5 million plunder.

What if your archeology field class was hiding assassins and dealers in black-market treasure?

Owen discovers a murdered corpse at a college-run archeological dig in the Utah outback but when he and a park service pilot try to reach the sheriff for help, their plane is shot from the sky. Owen must ditch the aircraft in the Colorado River, where he is saved by a moonshining hermit named Relic. The two flee from the sniper and circle back to warn the students. They must trek through rugged canyon country, unravel a baffling mystery, and foil a remarkable form of thievery. Suzy, a student at the dig, helps spearhead their escape but the unique team of crooks has a surprise for them…

Grand Master Adventure Writers' Finalist Award 2020

"Another gripping Relic tale with trademark wit and deft expression"

– Jacob P. Avila, Cave Diver, Grand Master Adventure Writers' Award Winner

"[A] humorous, fun, and well-plotted adventure,"

– Landon Beach, Bestselling author of The Sail, Grand Master Adventure Writers' Finalist Award

Onlinebookclub.org Review:

Wings offers "...action-packed adventure and nerve-racking suspense, with a touch of romance and humor mixed in"

Baldwin has a "gift for capturing the reader's attention at the beginning and keeping them spellbound"

Wings has "lots of thrilling action and twists"

Five Star Rating from Readers' Favorite:

"Wings… is a beautifully written thriller" with "funny, zippy dialogue"

"[The] plot is lively and exciting"

"suspense and action…keep[s] readers turning the pages until the very end."

"A quirky mix of adventure, mystery and the great outdoors" and "totally mad chase scenes… sure to be a hit with lovers of ancient history and crime thrillers alike."

DIAMONDS OF DEVIL'S TAIL

A moonshining hermit.
An English major.
A $4 million jewel heist.

When diamonds appear in a remote canyon stream, whitewater rafters and artifact thieves set off in a deadly race to the source.

Brayden, an aspiring writer, works in a Chicago insurance firm with his ambitious uncle when they embark on a wilderness whitewater adventure. On a remote hike, they find their colleague, Dylan, dead in the sand, a handful of gems in his fist. When thieves charge in, Brayden flees deeper into the canyon, where he encounters a gin-brewing recluse named Relic. Brayden's uncle is cornered and cuts a deal with the thieves, but they each have a surprise for the other… and the rafters have ideas of their own about getting rich quick… Brayden and Relic must become allies, traverse the harsh desert, and beat the thieves to the hidden gems. Brayden must confront his uncle about suspicious payments at their insurance firm and what he was really doing at the stream where Dylan was killed…

Can they discover the truth, find the lost jewels, and protect the rafters from grenade-tossing thieves?

Five Star Rating from Readers' Favorite:

"The excitement and tension are superb"

"…the entire plot [is] compelling"

"…an adeptly written thriller…"

Onlinebookclub.org four out of four Star Review:

"a rollercoaster ride of adventure, with multiple twists and turns, until the captivating end."

"straightforward and thrilling, with humor intermixed in the dialogue"

"Relic is a unique and intriguing character." "Relic is passionately interested in preserving the ancient archeological sites and conserving the land and water."

"[We] enthusiastically recommend it to readers who enjoy thrillers, action-packed adventure, and crime novels."

"Another rollicking Relic ride from A.W. Baldwin. This time, a bunch of double-crossing, dirt dealing, diamond thieves run into Relic's trademark wit and ingenuity. Enjoy!"

– Jacob P. Avila, *Cave Diver*, Grand Master Adventure Writers Award Winner

A.W. BALDWIN

DIAMONDS OF DEVIL'S TAIL

This is a work of fiction. The characters, incidents, and dialogues are products of the author's imagination and are not to be construed as real. Any resemblance to actual events or persons, living or dead, is entirely coincidental.

ISBN 978-1-7353626-0-1 Hardbound
ISBN 978-1-7353626-1-8 Paperback
ISBN 978-1-7353626-2-5 eBook

Cover art by Daniel Thiede.
Map art by Nate Baldwin.

For Gina

River
Ivan's camp
Pool
Stream
Boulders
Rafter's camp

Relic's
1st camp
Devil's
Tail
Stream
Hoodoos
Relic's
2nd
camp
Ridge
Plateau
N
W
E
S

CHAPTER 1
1957

Tommy stared at the third-story window across the street and launched a surge of smoke through his nostrils, cigarette pinched the way he held his guitar pick. He tossed the smoldering butt to the pavement and swallowed hard.

The hour had arrived.

The Southwest Jewelers' building was a rough redbrick, two decades old, its high, stately windows framed in black-painted pine. The nearest streetlight was around the corner, casting a sallow glow that ended where the road met the alley.

He was in the town of Cortez, named after the conquistador, one of the most brazen thieves in all of history, and the connection seemed fitting.

He tightened his cotton knapsack and sprinted toward the building, hopping as quietly as he could onto the first-story windowsill. His right hand slid along the wooden frame to the top, and he pulled himself up an inch and swung his left hand higher so that he hung onto the upper part of the frame, his feet dangling loosely beneath him. He did an awkward chin-up then slid one elbow over the top of the wide frame and rested a beat. He moved his other elbow onto the frame then reached above his head and into a crack between the bricks, a bit below the second-story window, his future balancing on his fingers.

This would be the trickiest part.

There was room enough for only four fingertips on the sharp edge of the brick. He lifted as much of his weight as he could on one arm and pushed with his other, slowly raising his stomach above the first-story window frame. He slapped his other hand into the crack between the bricks to his left, but an outward momentum suddenly threatened to toss him away from the wall and back to the hardened ground. He pulled even harder with his fingers against the brick, twisted his body closer to the wall, pulling, grunting, raising his waist, sliding his right toe onto the top of the frame, slowly, slowly stabilizing the tug of his weight. He held his body on the side of the wall just above the first floor window, his left leg dangling under him.

Thump! His left toe touched the glass on the

first-story window below.

Damn it. He swung his foot outward, away from the pane. If he broke it, that would be the end of this endeavor. And a fall from here would easily break his leg or his ankle, and escape would be a futile thought, smoke in the wind. Why hadn't he stolen a ladder for this?

No sounds came from inside the building.

He slid his right hand higher and felt the bottom of the second-story windowsill. He moved his left hand quickly to the sill and forced his fingers to hold him through another chin-up. He moved his elbows onto the bottom of the second-story window and rested a moment, his legs again dangling beneath him.

He slipped his right hand up along the side of the window frame, squeezed tightly, and lifted his left foot onto the sill beneath. Breathing hard, he pulled his other foot up and rose onto his toes until he could reach the top. Once there, he swung his left hand up, did another chin-up past the glass, and slid his elbows onto the top of the second-story window frame.

This would be the riskiest part.

With both hands, he reached for a crack in the brick and pulled carefully upward, relaxing his legs as they dangled above the second-story window. He tensed in another chin-up and quickly reached his right hand to the bottom of the third floor window, but it suddenly slipped from the frame and all of his weight balanced on the fingers of his left hand, crammed between the bricks. Though he'd practiced the maneuver before, his hand was straining, shaking, slipping inexorably from the crack. He knew he had but one chance and threw his right hand up again and onto the windowsill and dug into it with his fingernails, holding, holding until his left hand stabilized and he was hanging there like a spider on the wall. He pulled another chin-up and reached his left arm onto the sill and, from there, lifted himself and scrambled up, knees now resting on the wooden windowsill, sweat rolling from his forehead.

He reached into his pocket for a handkerchief and wrapped it around his hand, positioned it directly outward from the iron window latch and struck the glass with a muffled *crunch!*

The window broke inward. He gently pushed the shards inside until he could reach the metal latch. Anchored there, he stood carefully on the edge of the sill. His fingers pried the mechanism downward and the window opened quickly, pushing him outward and away from the wall, but he held onto the frame with his wrapped hand and swung past the opening window so he was standing before the darkened room.

Shish!

His muscles seized in place at the sound of metal on metal. The guard must have heard something – he'd slid open the first-story window. Slowly, carefully, Tommy turned his head and glanced down. The guard was peering out, looking for something, anything, that could have caused a sound. This was why Tommy hadn't stolen a ladder for the job – any noise, any passerby, any sudden urge from the guard to look out a window and the ladder would be a beacon, a silent alarm bringing all the other alarms and the police, and his hopes would be crushed.

His friend Will had made him abandon the idea, too.

He held his breath.

Please, please do not look up…

The guard grunted and pulled his head back inside. Tommy heard the first-story window slide shut and lock.

He took a deep breath of air. He pulled himself into the third-story room, careful to avoid stepping on the broken glass. He bent at the waist, shook out his fingers, loosened his muscles.

God, he could use another cigarette. But that would have to wait.

He slipped off his pack, reached for the flashlight, and crossed the open space to a stack of small wooden drawers, all labelled with numbers he did not understand. None of them were locked.

Tommy peered into the top drawer and his breath got stuck halfway up his throat.

CHAPTER 2

Diamonds spread across the bottom of the coffer, glistening under the light of his lantern. His fingers rolled across the tops of them, swirling them against the bottom of the drawer and he stared at them, wondering at their sparkle, guessing at their value, their wealth warming his belly.

"Must be a hundred thousand dollars..." he whispered to himself. "In this bin alone..."

He turned and pulled a tin cigar box from his pack and began scooping gems into the container, which he'd lined with felt. He moved quickly to the next drawer, and the next, gathering diamonds and colored gems of all sorts, rubies maybe, emeralds, sapphires, all cut and unmounted, polished and ready for setting into jewelry of all manner and make. He began to bounce on the balls of his feet, twisting in a barely restrained dance of joy as he emptied all eight tiny drawers, filling three sturdy tins to the brim. His sister's friend was married to the guard on duty tonight. Her whispered stories of the wealth in this room had been grossly understated.

Stay focused, he told himself.

He unwound a quarter-inch hemp rope from his knapsack and placed the boxes of gems into a sack inside his pack. He re-shouldered the pack and searched for something solid to tie onto. Cardboard boxes lined one wall along with a row of wooden chairs. The drawer with the gems in it was too small, too lightweight to use as an anchor. He went to the window and tied the rope to the iron latch. That ought to do it.

Tommy glanced below and stepped out onto the ledge.

He played out the rope until he stood horizontally against the outer brick wall, like he'd seen the army rappelers do, and walked his way down, one careful step at a time. He stopped at the first-story window and glanced in. All dark.

He stepped down to the ground and away from the building, his shoes crunching gravel.

A dangling rope would raise suspicion but, hopefully, would not be seen until morning. He and Will would be long gone by then, and not by any normal route.

Suddenly, light blasted its way into his periphery,

glowing from inside the first floor window.

Shit.

"Hey!" the window squealed open quickly and the guard poked his head through, peering directly at Tommy.

For a second, neither man moved.

The guard dove through the open window, arms and head first, summersaulting onto the ground.

Tommy turned and sprinted toward the alley.

"Get back here!"

He could hear the guard's boots scraping across the ground, speeding faster as he came.

"Thief!"

Tommy sped across the alley, away from the streetlight, past a clapboard building and onto Jefferson Street.

Bang!

The guard was shooting at him!

He fled across another alley and ran close to the buildings as a curve in the street gave him some quick cover. He poured all of his energy into his legs, pumping his feet across the tarmac, past a parked Dodge sedan, past the Interstate Bank building, then out in the open, to the other side of Jefferson Street, mindless panic heaving through his lungs.

"Hey!"

He turned past the hardware store and down another alley, the guard now out of sight but his footsteps coming hard. He ran past Rudd's place, then Lichtenfels', grateful for the darkened residential streets.

Bang!

Could the guard still see him?

Dogs began to whine and bark. A light popped on in the upper window next door as Tommy hopped a fence and cut through the back yard.

A donkey began to bray and it seemed the whole neighborhood would soon be awake and chasing him through the grass and into his dreams, churning ever closer, turning them into nightmares.

He glanced behind him but could not find the guard.

He hopped the rear fence and ran into a field of hay, part of it cut for the coming winter. He trotted across the open ground as fast as he dared, making his way by memory, leaving his flashlight in his pack. He came to a small ditch and hopped across, then made his way through uncut grass and a row of young cottonwoods. Another field opened before him and he could sense the silhouette of their transport and he began to sprint again. In minutes, he reached the airplane.

"Hey, slow down!" Will raised and lowered

his palms.

"I got it, Will, I got it all!"

"Lower your voice..."

Tommy grabbed Will by the arms and jumped up and down, pulling them both in a little dance.

"Great, great, great, great!" Will pulled himself away. "Now let's get going."

More dogs howled and distant lights flashed on, marking the guard's progress as he fumbled toward them.

Tommy turned toward the old Aeronca Chief, still hopping up and down.

"Toss the bag in back and strap in." Will stepped to the front of the plane and spun the propeller. He'd already turned on the ignition and blocked the left tire with wood, a method pilots used when they flew by themselves. The engine started right away, the prop spinning casually, kerchunk, kerchunk, kerchunk, the sound of the exhaust banging as it should.

"Hell, yeah." Tommy placed his pack behind the seats and hopped in.

Will removed the wooden block from the tire and tossed it next to the knapsack. He slid into his seat and buckled up. Tommy knew that at dusk Will had walked the farmer's road where they'd stashed the plane, making sure no worrisome rocks or holes presented themselves, then positioned the plane down the middle of the make-shift airstrip, an acre of tall, uncut hay on either side of them. Will knew to keep the plane on that heading until they'd lifted off. Still, taking off in the dark was a leap of faith…

Tommy looked behind them and saw a pin prick of light scan the sky maybe seventy yards away, coming through the cottonwoods, growing brighter. The guard had fallen behind, but he hadn't quit. Tommy turned back and stared at Will as he worked the throttle.

The engine strained and pulled and they bumped over the ground slowly at first then faster, faster, into the blind dark, the uneven dirt jarring their eyeballs and teeth, their hearts pinned to a simple belief in their flying machine until they lifted from the ground and into the sudden smoothness of flight. Tommy held onto his seat and decided not to look back again.

The Aeronca could easily fly ninety miles an hour, and Will set their course to the northwest, skirting west of the massive Rocky Mountains, aiming for the Colorado River, where, after sunrise, they could fly by sight northward and, after stops to refuel, on into Canada.

They'd done it! They'd really done it, Tommy thought. No more empty wallets, no more half-assed jobs cleaning horse stalls or flipping pancakes. He reached for

Will's shoulder and shook it gently.

"Wo-hoo!" Will shouted over the engine.

They hoped the police would think they'd made a mad dash by car into Mexico, the shortest path out of the country. But even if the guard realized they'd escaped by air, there was still no hint of their route, no way to track them through the night. No one could find them now. Not for a very long time, he thought.

And he would be right.

CHAPTER 3
PRESENT DAY

"Wicked chickens lay deviled eggs, but this one's rotten, too." Relic took the binoculars from his eyes and stroked his buffalo-beard goatee. Something about the man on the trail below made his skin tingle.

He slid away from the edge, out of the man's line of sight, and looked about. An unlikely descendant from clans of the Hopi and Scottish, Relic wandered the remote reaches of the Green and Colorado Rivers and the high plateaus between them, a weathered hermit at home in the desert outback, roaming ancient trails, brewing his homemade gin at a couple of narrow, spring-fed crags tucked above the floodplains. He tightened his ponytail, errant strands of white flashing through his coal-black hair.

A dried-out branch of cottonwood leaned against the nearest in a row of six Pueblo houses nestled tightly between the floor and ceiling of the cliff, a string of separate rooms, their stone blocks still mortared together in the corners. Inside were mano stones, held in the hand for grinding corn, and metate, wide-bottom slabs used for the same purpose. A child's bow and arrow, chert for making knives and arrowheads, and bowls of corn, squash, and other seeds were set neatly on indoor ledges under a layer of dust; their owners, it seemed, only away for the winter. In the farthest room was a row of large pots painted with white and black bolts of lightning, edges curved and sharp, with handles on their sides, tops still sealed tight, their contents a thousand year-old mystery. Relic meant to keep it that way.

He leaned forward again. The man strode purposefully toward the high cliff with something long, something strangely out of place, glinting in the desert sun. He put the binoculars back to his eyes.

Of all the things to be lugging in this remote country, to be balancing on bony shoulders in the noonday heat, that angular, outrageous shape was an aluminum ladder, designed for the suburban handyman.

"Well, shit on a shingle." Relic tucked the binoculars away, lay flat near the ruins, and waited.

The man struggled awkwardly up the trail, finally dragging the extension ladder to a stop at the base of the sandstone cliff. He wiped the sweat from his forehead and gazed upward at the solid, sloping rock and the extreme measures the Pueblo people had taken to keep their houses and granaries hidden and safe, high in the cliffs and crags, deep in the desert outback. Centuries ago, they carried masonry, mortar, and jars of water up rickety, wooden ladders to build these solid structures; hard, hot work with just one purpose – protection against interlopers. Now the man below had a ladder of his own, and he rested it against the stone and tugged on the rope that extended it upward, the arms squealing in their tracks, each rung clunking into place as it went.

The man shifted an empty duffle bag across his shoulders and began climbing carefully, one step at a time.

The twenty-eight foot ladder shifted suddenly an inch to the side, but it seemed to find a new, more solid base. The man flexed his knees, testing to make sure the aluminum would not slide any farther, and glanced up. The top of the ladder reached just above the lip of the sandstone ledge.

That man must think he'll find a load of artifacts up here, Relic thought, maybe even lower them to the ground by rope from the ruins, then step back down the ladder unencumbered. But the ancient Pueblo had one last line of defense.

Relic rolled away from the ruins and shifted along the ledge until he was directly in front of the top rung of the ladder, waiting. He listened as the man placed one hand on the step above him, then the next, one at a time, rising cautiously higher.

The man reached the cap of the ledge, but when he looked across the level shelf, where the stone walls rested, there, alone in the red dust, sat Relic looking, he knew, like a weathered Pueblo man, a ghost of the ruins, with a black goatee and a pony tail, holding a three foot cottonwood branch as thick as his arm.

"Shit!" the man's foot slid off one rung and down to the next. "Holy mother…who the hell are you?"

Relic's dark eyes squinted, his lips rose at the corners, and he slid the branch toward the man's ladder.

"What the hell?" the man tightened his grip.

Relic placed the branch on the top rung and began to push.

"No! Shit, no!" He raised his hand for a flash then returned it to the ladder. "You'll kill me!"

Relic slowly pushed the ladder away from the ledge, forcing it to twist outward on one end, then the other, as it lifted from the face of the cliff.

The man dropped both feet to the lower rung and slid his hands quickly down the aluminum sides, dropping his feet, holding for a moment, dropping, holding, dropping as the ladder leaned farther and farther away from the cliff, more and more upright above, ready to catapult him into a pile of rocks, and just as his feet hit the dirt the ladder tipped past its balance, dipped overhead and spun out of his hands and onto the rocky ground with a *clang,* a bounce, and another *clang!*

CHAPTER 4

Brayden followed his uncle Henry into the massive foyer at Reilley Tower, their dress shoes clacking against the terrazzo floor. Henry was an insurance agent at Olafsen and Wiles, a mid-sized firm specializing in policies for importers, shippers, and other regional companies. The firm occupied the entire sixth floor, with views overlooking the Chicago River.

"Hey, Henry, check it out..." Brayden pointed to a skinny-legged card table and a homemade sign near the elevators. Three hair-tousled eight-year-olds, one girl and two boys, sat behind a hand-painted box marked "cool aid," their smiles shy and fleeting, their eyes full of pent up energy. A pitcher of neon fluid and a row of paper cups sat expectantly on the table.

Brayden walked up to them. "How much?"

The middle child straightened her back. "Fifty

cents each," she announced.

"I'll take two." Brayden handed them a dollar and took two cups.

"Thank you, mister," she smiled, and the other two added their own thanks and nods.

Brayden handed one cup to Henry, and they stepped into an open elevator.

"You know…" Henry gazed into the artificially colored fluid, "someone should explain to them this stuff is toxic."

"Oh, come on, Henry, they're having fun."

"Then someone should explain they are actually selling cuteness, not something we should really drink."

"Cynic."

"No, I admire their drive. You have to take it to make it. But they think they're selling Kool-Aid, which means they will never maximize their potential."

Ding! The door slid open to the front office of Olafsen and Wiles, and they shuffled through a glass entrance that lead to rows of chest-high cubicles on their right and plush, inner offices on their left.

Brayden swallowed the neon fluid in one quick gulp. He watched Henry reach toward a potted palm and dump his Kool-Aid in the dirt.

Henry was a vigorous man in his fifties with short-cropped, graying hair and sharp brown eyes, always talking finances and dreaming of retirement. Six months ago, he'd married Brayden's aunt, Adel, a family centerpiece, a buoyant, affectionate woman who loved to walk and paint along the shores of Lake Michigan, a counterweight to her ambitious husband. The family slowly accepted the whirlwind romance, at least on the surface, but Brayden's mother, Adel's younger sister, quietly resisted it.

Last year, Brayden had begun writing a novella, scribbling while his college roommate slept, plotting while tedious professors droned along. A manic creativity carried him forward, but eventually he'd tossed it out as trash. He'd just completed his bachelor's degree in English at the University of Illinois and went promptly to the unemployment line. Until, that is, Uncle Henry hired him as a client representative – someone who handled phone calls, researched policy terms, answered questions, helped with group presentations. Henry could be a bore sometimes, but he was family now, and Brayden reminded himself that he appreciated the job and Henry's efforts to train him about all things financial. He needed to know about such things, didn't he?

Henry had won some sort of sales competition last fall, earning him two airline tickets and two seats on a guided, whitewater river trip in Utah. Aunt Adel swore she could doggie paddle, but that was it. The thought of falling into class III whitewater rapids was too much for her, she said, so she declined to join the trip. Henry invited Brayden to go in her place.

"Brayden!" Dylan strode toward them. "What's happening today?"

"Nothing new."

Dylan and Henry nodded to each other.

Dylan was only a few years older than Brayden, an up-and-comer at the agency with a keen competitive drive. He'd won second place in the same sales competition that Henry had won, earning Dylan one airline ticket and a seat on the same whitewater river trip.

"Ready to fly out this afternoon?" Dylan glanced at each of them and smiled an even row of teeth. "White water?"

"Sure." Brayden nodded, but, really, he wasn't sure at all. He couldn't do much more than a doggie paddle himself, and the idea of crashing through whitewater rapids seemed more foolhardy than fun. But his aunt had put her warm hand on his arm and implored him to keep Henry company, to help watch over him during the trip. Henry seemed vaguely amused at the idea that the excursion could be dangerous and considered it to be some sort of personal challenge for Brayden – would he go or wimp out? Eventually, he'd decided not to disappoint Aunt Adel. And not to embarrass himself.

"Yes." Henry gave a thumbs up.

"Hey, can you look at a draft report for me?" Dylan asked Brayden.

"Sure."

"I emailed it to you. Could use a little more skill with the English language than I have to offer." Dylan grinned.

"You bet."

"See my new sales numbers?" Dylan turned to Henry.

"Yes, Dylan, pretty impressive." Henry's lips pulled back from his teeth in a half-hearted smile.

"Watch out, old man," Dylan teased, poking a finger at him, "or I'll be passing you in the left lane pretty soon."

"Right you are." Henry rubbed his neck as if he'd just had a sudden crick in it.

"Grab your files and let's get across the street." Dylan pointed toward the Howell Building. "We have that 8:30 meeting with Schweitzer, remember?"

"Right," Henry turned toward Brayden. "Finish up the quarterly report, would you? Double check it against the numbers on my desk. There's an open file…"

"Got it."

"Let's get some coffee first," Henry said as they walked toward the coffee cart. "I can't take a whole morning of Schweitzer without a dose of caffeine..."

Brayden settled into his chair and clicked a command to print a draft of the quarterly report. He retrieved it from the printer and reviewed the paragraph introducing the subject: first quarter on-going sales, new sales, revenue, all compared to the first quarter a year ago. But as he studied the numbers on the pages that followed, the dip in employees this year seemed too dramatic to be correct. Better check the numbers again, he thought.

Brayden went to his uncle's office, a spacious, private room with a view of downtown, and went inside, checking the top of the desk for last year's report. Nothing obvious, except that it's a mess. He smiled at a picture of his beaming aunt on the side bookshelf and turned back to the desk. The main computer screen was dark, a laptop situated in front of it, phone message-slips spread across an "in" box. He lifted letters, notes, papers, file folders, and a legal pad, but saw nothing with the numbers he needed. Should he check Henry's computer? He'd be gone until lunch and Brayden needed to finish his review this morning so Henry and Dylan could finalize it by 1:30p.m. They had a whitewater trip to get to.

He sat in Henry's chair and searched for the mouse to the large computer, with no luck. He touched the pad on the laptop and the screen lit up – a sunset view of Henry and Aunt Adel on Henry's sailboat on Lake Michigan. He scrolled to the directory and began to scan the titles. The files were named without vowels, so "report" was "rprt" and "contacts" was "cntcts" but some files even omitted random consonants, so he guessed that "mgt" was "management" and "prsn" was "personnel." He tried to open the "prsn" file, but it wanted a password. Crap. Why would Henry password protect these? Maybe they were individual employee files, confidential ones Brayden did not really want to see. But he needed to check, so, he thought, try Aunt Adel's name. He tried her full name and then her maiden name without success. It must be a company-wide password, something to do with the date it was established or some other business related thing that Brayden would never guess. He should ask the ladies at the front desk – someone in the office would have it. But then he tried Adel's birthday and it popped right open. Within it were several sub-files, none of which made any sense, names like "lttl" and "st" and "tbl." Brayden began with "st."

All the documents were listed by number. The first one showed a transfer of $155,000 from the Shoreline

Transportation Company in Chicago to a bank with an address in Montreal. The transfer referenced claim number 99854, a claim made to Brayden and Henry's employer, Olafsen and Wiles.

He opened the next one, and the next, each showing payment by Shoreline Transportation in various amounts over the last four years: $140,000; $77,500; $134,600; and so forth, and each with policy dates, claim dates, and payment dates. Were they Henry's sales commissions? Wouldn't they be paid by the company, not the customer?

The hairs on his arm began to rise and he knew he should not be in these files; they were not the employment numbers he wanted, they were nothing he wanted to see at all, but he stared at the next folder on the list, the one labelled "tbl," and he couldn't help himself. Just one little click, he thought, and he was inside the folder and found the same numbered list of documents, nothing to show what they might be. He opened the first one: $144,200 from Table Island Contractors to the same bank in Montreal; then $57,000; then $48,800; then $72,300. Finally, he stopped clicking on the documents and sat back into Henry's chair, staring at the screen. Something about the dates of the policies, claims, and payments bothered him.

"Sir?" It was Susan's voice, crisp and polite, in the hall outside.

"Forgot my notes from the last meeting." Henry was hurried, slightly out of breath as he passed Susan and moved into view, directly toward his open office door.

Brayden's chest seemed to grind slowly at first, hot metal on metal, then the piston fired and he gasped and shifted forward instinctively, reaching for the mouse pad.

Henry was now only a few steps away.

Brayden slid his fingers quickly, aiming and clicking, aiming, missing the damned icon, come on, come on, come on, aiming again and clicking, clicking, retreating from the files like they were flames licking at his fingers and he closed the laptop screen just as Henry walked into the office.

"Find what you need?" Henry went to his desk and picked up a legal pad with notes on it.

"No, not yet." Brayden needed a deep gulp of air that he could not seem to get. What if Henry remembered that he'd left his computer screen on?

"Here..." Henry kept his eyes on the desk and pushed a folder towards Brayden. "Here are the numbers you need." He looked up for a moment and seemed to stare at Brayden a little too long.

"Thanks." Brayden found a shallow breath of air,

grabbed the folder, and rose from the chair.

"Sure." Henry's voice sounded tentative, or was it Brayden's imagination? "Gotta run." Henry turned and moved quickly out of the office and down the hall, out of sight.

Brayden just stood there in Henry's office, folder dangling from his hand, breathing through his mouth.

CHAPTER 5

Relic heard the man cursing and stomping the ground below.

"What the hell is wrong with you? What the hell are you doing up there?"

Relic slid back toward the ruins and the cliff that cradled them, farther out of sight.

"Gawdamnit!"

He heard the man struggling with the aluminum ladder, so he slid to the edge again and peered over. Ladder man raised a middle finger toward the top of the cliff and mumbled a curse. Then he wrestled the thing to its shorter length, lifted it, and balanced it on his shoulders. He began to stumble cautiously over the rocks and brush, back the way he'd come.

Relic raised binoculars to his eyes and studied the man's clumsy trek toward the river. There, in the direction he was heading, floated two blue rafts, nearly hidden along the shore. A flash of light there meant others were waiting nearby. But the ladder man seemed to have given up. If he was going to bring more people here to loot the ruins, he would not have carried his ladder away.

The man disappeared behind a ridge and reappeared below it, farther along a little trail toward the river. What were they doing here? Trolling for artifacts? Or was the man's excursion to this ruin a one-time whim?

No. No one brought a ladder on a rafting trip without the intent to reach places that might have valuable Pueblo tools, weapons, clothing, and maybe even, he shuddered, burial sites. The ladder man was a thief, intent on what he was doing, and he had some help from the other rafters.

Relic watched as the man reached the blue boats. He could not hear them but could see all three of them setting the aluminum across the middle of the closest raft, the ends of the ladder hanging even with the sides of the dinghy. They busied themselves with other packing, which meant they'd eventually be back in the current of the wide, brown river.

Side canyons and tributaries of this great watercourse held hundreds of Pueblo ruins, some nearly pristine, some worn down to their foundations. The next drainage downriver was Hangman Canyon, a rough, wide plain with old uranium mines, active during the 1950s. Hangman had no Pueblo pictographs, ruins, or burials, but the ladder man might not know that – he might spend a day or two there searching. After Hangman came a deeper canyon that ran west along a tiny creek to a light fall of water and a wading pool. Beyond that, a side canyon forked north, twisted to the west, then stopped at an arrowhead-shaped gorge with no way out. The unique shape gave the whole place its name – Devil's Tail Canyon. Farther up the main drainage, past the distinctive side canyon, hid a high castle of stone inserted on a ledge twenty-five feet above ground level. The ruin had three distinct stories, wooden beams still in place for the floors of the upper rooms, an area still virtually undisturbed.

Relic lowered his binoculars and sat for a moment. The ruins next to him were hard to reach and off the beaten path, successfully protected by federal law and the National Park Service. He glanced above at the fire-blackened roof of the cliffs and could almost smell turkey and maize in the cooking pots. An old corn grinding song arose in his head, one his great aunt had sung back on the mesa.

He tucked his binoculars into his pack and found

the rope he'd used to descend to the ruins from the cliff above. He climbed the first five feet hand over hand up the rope, then carefully along a crack in the sandstone to a higher ledge, and to another, until he reached the crest of the plateau above the old Pueblo townhouses. He untied his rope from an anchored boulder, rolled it up, and stuffed it into his pack. From there, he began a measured trot across hard, bare rock to the south, a path that would bring him downriver to Hangman Canyon then on to Devil's Tail, where those remote, virgin ruins could be the ladder man's next target.

CHAPTER 6

Em pulled her dark hair behind her ears and straightened papers on the conference room table. Her earthen eyes squinted when she listened, her dimpled smile magnetic, a distinctive, slender gap between her two front teeth. A degree in geology and a master's in outdoor recreation, she'd landed her job at Save Our Canyons and moved from Laramie, Wyoming, just two weeks before. The organization dedicated its efforts to protecting wilderness areas in the southwest, particularly the river and canyon country where their offices were located. Her boss, a resolute, old-school codger, moved the organization forward with a combination of military discipline and arm-twisting politics. He'd built the non-profit from a small group of environmentalists in the 1990s into a coalition of concerned citizens, recreation industry retailers, and outdoor therapy professionals. Em's first key task on the job was to spend five days on a whitewater river trip, getting to know some of the country first-hand.

She looked forward to it.

Her boss stepped into the conference room and nodded a quick greeting. He pointed a remote at the television and clicked his way to the video conference call he'd scheduled that morning. The finance officer and administrator shuffled in behind him, coffee mugs in hand, and they all settled in for the call.

The screen flickered for a moment and a man in his sixties appeared, his pale head balding, his suit a slick navy-black, wire-rimmed glasses perched on his nose. Intense and intelligent, his eyes scanned Em and the others. They quickly introduced themselves to each other.

"Everyone," their boss looked around the room, "I've asked Mr. Chatsworth, of the D.C. firm of Gaub and Mead, to spend some time with us this morning to discuss the kind of effort we need to defeat recent changes in mining and drilling regulations and efforts to open parts of Bears Ears and Canyonlands to oil and gas development. Even more critical is how climate change is affecting river flows and springs and the need for new rules to help mitigate that. You're all aware of the environmental and degradation risks to these wilderness areas, so I want to focus today on what it will take for us to get more politically active on the federal level, not just generally as we are now but specifically to try to address these unfortunate developments." He held a palm toward the screen. "I've had several calls with Mr. Chatsworth about the work we do here, the importance of our relationship with the canyons and rivers, and I've asked him to give us a frank briefing about what would be needed..."

Chatsworth cleared his throat. "Thanks for setting up this call today. For those who don't know me, I've been active in running political campaigns and lobbying, mostly on the east coast, for nearly forty years. A non-profit like yours tends to hire lobbyists who have a relationship with the great outdoors, like you do, but that's a mistake. Don't let anyone fool you. What you really need is someone with political relationships in Washington, D.C. And in case you haven't already noticed, I have a tendency to be brutally direct with my clients, and potential clients like Save Our Canyons."

"We like that," the boss nodded.

"Well, then, let's get right to it." Chatsworth placed his hands together as if in prayer. "I've reviewed the new regulations and must say this: it's always harder to reverse something than it is to stop it in the first place. Same is true with federal legislation. There are a hundred ways to stop it. Getting something passed is the real trick in this town. So with respect to the new oil drilling regulations, we would be starting from behind.

"Also, you must grab the ear of the key players in this business," he tugged his right lobe, "and you don't get that just by asking. I don't mean to insult anyone in this meeting, but I have to say that most legislators could give a rat's ass about hiking or camping in the hot, sweaty, dirty out-of-doors."

They all glanced at each other.

"I know it's your passion, but most people who run the government didn't get here because they love the planet. So how do you get congressmen and women and senators to care about your cause? You have to make common cause with them, find what they already care about and join with them, partner with them, so they will see you as a friend, an ally."

"And how do we do that, exactly?" The boss leaned forward.

"You absolutely must contribute to the political campaigns of Senators Williams, Cox, Black, and probably Lopez. Each one chairs or actively leads the key committees of jurisdiction that will affect your efforts. Then, you'll need to contribute handsomely to representatives on each of the House committees of jurisdiction, eight of them in all. This will be in addition to generous donations to your own congressional delegation, of course." He placed his hands back on the table in front of him. "Money, folks. That's the basis of your common cause." He peered at them over silver-framed glasses.

Em bit the inside of her lip, disgusted by what they'd heard, upset by the truth she sensed within it.

"Don't shoot the messenger, folks." Chatsworth spread his hands wide.

"Anything else?" the boss asked with a hint of sarcasm.

"Not much point in anything else if you can't embark on this kind of financial commitment. But yes, there are about four specific tasks to undertake."

"Keep going…" the boss crossed his arms and sat back in the chair.

"First, if you hire me, I recommend that you hire someone in-house who can write well and quickly: press releases, letters seeking or expressing support, those sorts of things. I know you've done that on a piecemeal basis in the past, but you're going to have to prepare a lot more written material for representatives and senators and you'll have to prepare it quickly for long stretches of time. My firm can help guide this person. We have the public relations experience, so this individual should work to some extent under our review, subject to your final call on any decisions, of course.

"Second, you'll have to finance studies of the effects of these new regulations and climate change. That's something you could coordinate with other groups, pool your resources maybe. You also might be able to rely on existing research, which is another cost-saver.

"But here's the third thing you absolutely must have: an accurate poll in each of several key jurisdictions – where these key senators and representatives are from – that will catalogue public attitude about the environment or the areas you want to protect from the new regulations. If you don't know the concerns and attitudes of their constituents, you can't begin to influence their thinking, what positions their constituents will or will not support. And we can't just do something generic, like asking what people think about global warming. We need to know what the public would think if the rivers can't be rafted anymore or springs used by ranchers or wildlife dry up, those sorts of specific concerns.

"Finally, you need to upgrade your social media efforts big time to embark on a campaign to influence the constituents of each representative and senator we focus on, the ones who can herd special legislation along or kill any harmful regulatory changes."

Em felt herself bracing against the table, feeling the

weight of the work that would have to be done.

The boss clasped his hands together. "What would each of these steps cost, in rough estimates, do you think?"

Chatsworth looked up, figuring in his head. "Based on my experience, it will take close to seven hundred thousand a year to make the needed political contributions. Add another one hundred thousand for the impact study and political polling. Well, no, those could be more like three hundred thousand because you have polling to do in several states. The social media work is something our firm can do for you. If you hire me, and we also do that work, add another five hundred thousand for the start-up and first ninety day's work. After that, another fifty thousand a month, so, say close to another five hundred thousand to get you through the first year."

Em's stomach clenched.

"Holy..." the finance officer whispered. "Sorry," she added hastily.

"Two million, five..." The boss stared at Chatsworth from under his brow.

"That would provide a respectable effort, with a genuine chance for some success, yes."

CHAPTER 7

Deputy Dawson stroked his auburn mustache and stared at the topographic maps posted on the wide corkboard in his basement command center. He'd been forced to re-locate his maps and research here because Sheriff Meyers had insisted there was insufficient room at the station, and now Dawson's search for the elusive hermit of the Canyonlands had become a full-fledged, off-duty, police investigation.

He touched one of the blue push-pins that marked known water sources other than the Colorado or Green Rivers themselves: springs, creeks, or pools a moonshiner could use for distilling illegal gin.

There had been sightings of a recluse for years, particularly in association with archeological townhouses, kivas, and caches. Rumors spread that he sold moonshine for cash but avoided nearly everyone, especially law enforcement. Four years ago, a whitewater rafting group encountered grave diggers in search of artifacts to sell on the black market. Four people were murdered. One of the criminal defendants insisted he'd chased a man with a goatee who later overcame him and tied him up. One of the rafters said a rancher helped them, but he refused to give his name and left the scene before the sheriff arrived. But there were no haciendas and no grazing rights for ranchers anywhere near Horse Canyon. And the debacle in Raptor Canyon two years ago, where witnesses described a dark-skinned man with a ponytail monkey-wrenching the land development there, a fiasco that later revealed a $35 million con job. But no one on the construction crew had a ponytail. And the incident at Ghost Creek last year, where thieves claimed a student with a goatee fired a dozen rounds of ammunition at them, but none of the students ever had a goatee. No one seemed to have a name for this phantom or know why he had been at these places or where he'd gone when law enforcement arrived.

He must be found and detained for questioning. And maybe for prosecution.

Dawson reached behind him for another pin and it poked firmly into his finger.

Shit.

He swung his hand for a moment or two then pressed it against his leg.

Other officers teased him about his work, calling it a nit-witted search for bigfoot. Witnesses could be highly unreliable, they'd say, especially in circumstances like the ones involved. Indeed, some witnesses said there was no such man at all, while others described him as tall, short, long-haired, crew-cut, and so forth. But Dawson knew in his heart that this specter actually existed.

It seemed pretty unlikely that organized crime was directly involved, but, then again, he couldn't rule it out entirely. No one he knew was tough enough to traverse and survive these canyons undetected without help from somebody. Not that he would admit these private thoughts to anyone else, but the mob would love to embarrass law enforcement if it could, and this unsolved case was an awkward morass with plenty of potential for unwanted national attention. Some days, the case reeked of organized crime. Other days, mob involvement seemed pretty far-fetched. But when Dawson finally found his desert bigfoot, no one would be chuckling anymore. And the commissioner would award him a commendation.

He tied a line of yarn between the blue push-pins and marked a spot near the center of the string in a wide canyon along the river. He crossed his arms and stared at the maps.

This year, he was taking a more active approach.

CHAPTER 8

"Find anything?" Jebediah glanced up as Ivan neared the shore.

"Looked long and hard," Ivan lied, shaking his head. His encounter at the ruins had been creepy and alarming, his nerves still bruised from the scare. That guy in the Pueblo ruins had nearly killed him, shoving his ladder away from the cliff like that. It was a most unsettling reversal, and he was in no mood to share it with others. He unshouldered the aluminum ladder and laid it onto the ground. "Bare as day-after shelves in a food bank."

Jeb grunted.

Ivan lifted the baseball cap higher on his forehead and took a breath. A lanky six-foot-one, he wore his sleeves rolled up and his pants long and loose. His eyes scanned back and forth, glass-blue beads examining the riverbank. Sometimes Ivan worked on commission in auto sales, sometimes at the parts store, often spending long weekends at big-city flea markets or scouting historic sites to plunder. When the weather forecast for the week improved unexpectedly, this trip had come together at the last minute.

"I'd put my money on some of those side canyons in Devil's Tail." Jeb was a bear of a man, husky and muscled, quick to judge, little to fear. He'd joined the army at age nineteen, been accused of stealing ordnance when he was twenty-one, and discharged four months later amid unsubstantiated reports of an off base explosion. He and Ivan had met through a local black market dealer; Jeb trading in hand grenades, Ivan in museum quality artifacts. They'd hit it off.

"You may be right. But I want to hit Hangman Canyon first, along the way." He looked about. "Where's Barclay?"

"Screwing around somewhere." Jeb checked the rest of the gear.

"May as well get our butts downriver." Ivan lifted one end of the ladder and handed it to Jeb, who carefully pulled it across the metal frame of Ivan's raft and began lashing it down.

"My thinking too. We need to set up a new camp

for the night."

"Let's get the tents rolled up."

"Right." Jeb stepped from the raft.

Ivan tilted his head back and yelled: "Barclay!"

"Here!" A stocky man in a green T-shirt and gold and white baseball cap stepped from behind a rise and trotted quickly toward the camp. Barc and Ivan had worked together at a local car wash after high school, lost contact for a couple of years while Barc took engine repair classes in Durango, and they'd reconnected last fall. Just last month, Barc had robbed two convenience stores along Route 191 and was, as they say, laying low for a while. Personally, Ivan preferred to liberate goods where there were no cameras, alarms, or armed cashiers, but to each his own. Ivan had convinced Barc they might make some money on this trip if they could find some old Pueblo artifacts, and Barc had said, what the hell, why not tag along?

The three of them stood near their camp kitchen.

"That porta-potty tent is all yours." Barc pointed at the narrow white and orange tent staked around the camp toilet.

"Ha. Ha." Ivan wobbled his head. "I told you I won it at a raffle…"

Barc shrugged.

"...at the hardware store."

"Right."

Barc grinned and helped Jeb take down the rest of the tents. They carried their gear down to the water, where they had two twelve-foot rubberized rafts, one that belonged to Ivan, rigged to carry him, Barc, and the ladder, and one that belonged to Jeb. They soon had them all packed.

"Where to?" Barc asked.

Ivan hopped into the boat, unfastened his life preserver from the frame, and clipped it around his chest. "Past the bend. Hangman Canyon first, for the night, then on to Devil's Tail. We'll stay close to shore, on the left."

Barc nodded and Jeb pushed from shore with one of the oars.

"Let's avoid any other rafters, if we can," Ivan looked at Jeb.

"If we can." Jeb released a quick grin then lifted his seat pad and pointed. Ivan recognized the custom-made waterproof bag where Jeb kept his 9mm Smith and Wesson, a short-barreled, 469 pistol. He knew that Jeb was used to other people avoiding him.

CHAPTER 9

Brayden, Henry, and Dylan had flown into Moab, Utah, the night before, where they'd wandered the shops on Main Street, feeling the warm evening air. Brayden had found himself stealing glimpses of Henry whenever he wasn't looking, staring as if his face would miraculously reveal whatever secrets he had catalogued on his laptop, the names and payments and dates, and whether he suspected what Brayden had done, the records he'd seen. Brayden had tried to stop sneaking these glances at Henry, knowing the thought was absurd. The feeling was wholly irrational, like he was the one doing something wrong, something bad, as if the devil himself was going to flay him alive for it.

His acid reflux had flared.

But how would he be caught? Brayden had closed the files before Henry had come into the office, and he'd turned the computer back on, the way Henry had left it, before he'd returned to his desk at the cubicle. Still, he'd consumed more than one antacid that evening.

As the three of them chatted about workaday politics, management's newest missteps, Dylan's latest crush, Brayden had slowly pushed his fears, his questions, farther into the back of his mind, buried in the mundane. When they speculated about what their whitewater trip would be like, riding the rafts, Brayden had stopped obsessing about what was on Henry's computer – visions of seasickness and waterfalls became a new focus for his anxiety.

They'd awoken early to catch the long drive to their put-in spot on the river, where their guides lectured them on trip logistics and safety before they all climbed into their rafts. When they floated away, spinning lazily in the breeze, the lectures and the anxiety seemed to float away, too.

Now Brayden bit his lip and ran his fingers along the cotton rope that circled the whitewater craft, letting his uncle's words slide in and out of his attention. He glanced into the thin sky and back to the boat, nodding automatically.

"...avionics is the stock to buy, Brayden. It's solid, steady growth, I mean, think about it... Airlines and the technology to support them."

A stiff breeze carried Henry's words into a row of old cottonwoods to the side of the wide river, dissolving them into gibberish. Brayden shifted his seat on the side of the boat.

He'd bought a stenographer's pad the previous night, before they went back to the hotel, thinking he could do some writing on this trip, maybe keep a journal. Or try some poetry. To be successful, he'd have to give himself permission not to write anything at all so that, when the words did come, they were natural and unforced. That was his theory, anyway. But since his last writing project, a novella he eventually tossed in the dumpster, he'd suffered from persistent writer's block, unsure whether he could ever unclog it, uncertain what would happen if he did.

The gray raft flexed downward, straightening his knees as it floated over a set of ripples. He tugged a strap on the side of his life preserver, the device so tight he had trouble taking a deep breath.

His mind wandered to Caitlin, a cute social work major with librarian-frame glasses and a subtle smile. They'd dated a few times, dinner at Antonio's, movie night on campus, optimism carrying them farther into the relationship than it was really meant to go. Now that he was no longer on campus, he felt untethered, naked in the new world, familiar friends and romantic interests suddenly at a distance.

"…so, that's the point of it all, right?"

Brayden nodded absently.

The raft was not at all the squishy, rubbery thing he'd expected. Instead, it had a skeleton of sorts, a rigid wooden frame in the center where their guide, Connor, sat and rowed. And the boat was so tightly filled with air that its sides felt like a row of metal bleachers at a soccer game. Sleeping bags, tents, and supplies were packed into waterproof bags and lashed to the pine frame with straps and ropes. He and Uncle Henry sat in the front. Three other guests sat in the rear: Dylan, and Claire and Carl, who were together. They'd met quickly at the gathering where the guides had briefed them on safety protocols for the five day trip. In all, there were three guides, one for each raft, and ten guests.

Noise like an idling diesel reached his ears and at first he wondered where it was coming from, and then a thought crept into his head and his heart seemed to thump once hard against his ribs.

Connor had said that before they entered the rapids he would order them to squat low in the raft, hold the outer rope with one hand, and hold an inner rope secured to the wooden frame with the other. Connor's gaze was focused on the water, but he'd not alerted them yet.

Up ahead, the river turned sharply to their right and the ripples had turned choppy. They swept past the shore more quickly now, gathering speed, and suddenly they rounded the corner and the slow-rumbling diesel turned into a ramjet engine, roaring and wailing into the air with a force that vibrated the hair on his neck, and the water became a roiling series of waves splashing high into the air, dead ahead of them.

"Positions!" Connor set his feet hard against the wooden frame and began to pull on the oars.

Brayden slid to the floor of the raft, knees on the bottom, hands on the ropes, wishing now that his chest-strangling life jacket could be tightened again, just one last time, before he met the thundering waters.

"Oh, hell." Henry dropped to the bottom of the raft and grabbed the ropes.

Connor pulled deeply on the oars, tugging them slowly, slowly across the current toward the left-side shore.

Now the rapids roared like waterfalls, blasting all other sounds from the air, a crushing, claustrophobic force that muffled his ears, isolating him from everything and everyone else. Would they even hear a cry for help?

A trough appeared to his right as deep as a one-story

house, flowing at a sprinter's pace, and he turned straight ahead just as the nose of the raft rose quickly into the air, nothing before him but pale blue sky, and it seemed to hover, ever so briefly, at the top, then splashed through the wave and angled downward to the bottom of the trough, levitating his body until only his white-knuckled fingers held him inside the fragile raft, a carnival ride without gauges or speed limits or safety valves and his breath came only in short, rough, gasps.

They were instantly up again, rising on the next wave, water blasting his cheeks, shoving him back against the wooden frame, and he could barely see at all but could feel a new, centrifugal force swinging them to the right and another wall of water crashed against him and tore his hand from his inside grip and flipped him like a dishrag to the outside of the raft, his legs flailing, chest-deep in the rapids, left arm swinging for purchase and finding none, diaphragm taut against his ribs, throat choking on the churning water.

CHAPTER 10

Brayden sensed a pair of hands grab the top of his life preserver, and he squeaked upward across the rubber tube, over the top, and flopped awkwardly onto the floor of the raft, face down in a frigid puddle. He lifted his head, wiped the water from his eyes and squirmed about, searching for something to grasp.

"Hold on!" Connor turned from Brayden and hopped across the wooden frame, back into his seat between the oars. Brayden found a dry bag tied to the boat and wrapped his fingers around the ropes that anchored it.

The raft rose again, cramming his chest into the bag, then dropped, pulling him away, but Brayden kept a firm hold.

The boat rose and fell in shorter moves, evening out as the rapids resolved into calmer water. Brayden sat more upright and looked around.

"Close one there!" Henry nodded.

"Shit." Brayden took a deep breath and wiped his face. His hair felt matted in clumps, his chest tight and bruised. He'd been tossed from their raft as if by a flick of the wrist, and nearly lost to the roiling waves. Chilled river water weighed on his clothes like wet glue.

"Nice job." Connor spun them casually about. "You did just what you were supposed to do there, Brayden. Hold onto the ropes, stay by the raft, ride it out. We had a break in the waves, so I was able to pull you in before the last rapid."

Nice job, my ass, Brayden thought. I could have easily slipped off the raft entirely and been lost to the rapids. And drowned.

"Way to cool off." Carl gave him a friendly salute from the back of the boat.

Brayden forced a smile in return and faced forward, away from everyone, feeling the precious air in his lungs, expanding, expelling, suddenly aware how desperately he depended upon it, in every moment.

The wide river carried them gently now, toward towering sandstone cliffs on their left, past broken hills and a lonely spire to their right. The early summer sun began to dry and warm his skin, and he stared ahead, calming his nerves, regaining his sense of security in their sturdy rubber raft. The rapids had taken the spark out of Henry's diatribe, and they all floated quietly, Brayden thankful for the silence.

They rowed past narrow inlets and wide canyons, jostled through mild rapids, and spun gently in the breeze, staring at cliffs that towered above them, some rising from beneath the water line. Connor regaled them with tales of geologic history, the names and eons of layers upon layers of stone. They were drifting through a primeval realm, the birth and rise and death of dinosaurs, time slowing to something deep and prehistoric.

After several hours on the water, Connor rowed slowly toward the left shore, where a wide canyon opened before them. The river bent a little to the right, then rounded back toward the long canyon.

"This is Devil's Tail Canyon." Connor lifted the oars from the water. "We'll camp here tonight."

"Sounds good," Henry turned toward the canyon. "I'm beat."

"Tomorrow we'll hike up to a little waterfall and swim in the pool there, if there's enough water in it. There are also side canyons to explore if you like. It'll take most of the day, so we'll stay here tomorrow night, too."

They floated another hundred yards or more, and

Connor pulled on the oars again, scraping them across the sand to a sudden stop on the beach.

The other two rafts came ashore next to them, and the quiet air filled with happy chatter, clanking metal, guests splashing in the river. Connor led them into a "fireman" formation running from the rafts to the shade of two cottonwoods higher on the shore, and they ferried tents, food, sleeping bags, and other gear from one person to the next, piling it all in the shade of the trees. Brayden pulled off his life preserver and tied it with the others on a post marking their spot as "campground two," the second of two camps in Devil's Tail.

He found the dry bag that held his sleeping bag, pulled it aside, and sat on it. The river was peaceful here, a gentle flow of milk and coffee through layers of horizontal sandstone, banded in caramel and chocolate, rocks and more rocks, like he'd never imagined before. Across the water rose a solid wall of brick-colored cliff, polished by wind and water to a sheer, slick surface, blackened stains streaking from the rim, syrupy drizzle on a giant cake.

He removed his shirt and wrung the water out. It dried quickly in the breeze and he put it back on, but his cotton underwear was still cold and damp. He found the packed tent he would use and walked to a flat area past the trees and set it up. Then he found the dry bag with his clothes and sleeping bag and tossed it in the tent. Inside, he changed into dry pants and stretched out on the soft bag for a few moments, staring at the top of the tent, listening to bits and pieces of talk from the other campers.

Brayden relived the moment he was thrown from the raft and into the chaos and convulsion of the rapids, helpless against the cold current, no time to think or react or defend against the pandemonium. He had no time to see or calculate anything, just a flash-memory of himself whipping out of the raft, his face striking hard against the rubberized side, right hand gripping the safety rope, legs flailing beneath the boat. He felt a newfound respect for the unyielding power of the river and shuddered at what might have come to pass if he'd been fully ejected from the raft.

CHAPTER 11

A swelling hunger had driven Brayden out of this tent to mingle and eat. He couldn't help but notice the blonde in yellow shorts flirting with a guy from her raft, whom she seemed to know. A moment later she was tossing her spaghetti-straight hair at Connor and smiling a perfect row of white teeth.

He knew the names of their three guides: Connor, George, and Audrey. Connor was guide on the lead boat, the one Brayden shared with Henry, Dylan, and the young couple, Claire and Carl. George had the "supply boat" and no passengers. Audrey had five passengers too, including one woman, three middle-aged men who appeared to be friends, and the blonde. He'd forgotten their names promptly after they'd been introduced, a flaw in his mental capacity he found annoying. The guests all chattered in the cool evening air, moving from their camp chairs to the make-shift kitchen and back again, eating, refilling their plates, returning dirty dishes to the table.

He finished the last bites of his burrito and rice, a fine supper cooked by the crew on an open grill. The equipment they provided for the trip was impressive. Among other things, the rafts carried two long tables with legs that unscrewed for storage, two propane tanks, a metal cooking range, pots and pans, a sizeable cooler, tents, sleeping bags, folding chairs, wildlife guidebooks, a camp toilet, and even a portable bar. Packing it all into three whitewater rafts was an engineering feat.

"How about that for a meal?" Henry pulled up a chair next to Brayden's.

"Solid."

Henry nodded and leaned into Brayden. "Her name is Madison."

"Who?"

"The girl in the super-short 'hot' pants, over by the rafts. You should go chat with her, see what she thinks of the trip so far."

Brayden tightened his lips and stared at him.

"I'm just saying…" Henry shrugged. "You see an opportunity…You gotta take it to make it, you know." He rubbed a hand across his short-cropped hair.

Brayden looked to his feet and shook his head.

"Hey, boys." Dylan sauntered toward them. "Up for a game of horseshoes?" He patted his stomach and smirked like a cartoon cat that had cornered a mouse.

"Sure." Henry straightened in his seat. "Set us up."

"Fifty bucks a game?" Dylan challenged him.

"Hundred a game."

"You're on." Dylan turned and walked toward Connor, who was pounding iron stakes into the sand.

"Competitive bastard," Henry whispered to Brayden.

"You just doubled his bet!"

"Have to with Dylan or he'll steamroll you."

Brayden gave him a sideways look.

"Hey, be careful of that one at the office, Brayden. He'll stab you in the back for a half a sandwich." Henry rose and followed Dylan to the horseshoe game.

"Huh..." He thought about that for a moment.

The sun laid its head on a distant table-top, its heat enflaming the sky, its sideways glare tearing the cliffs into ragged shadows. Brayden stared upriver toward layers of rock on rock, grays on hazy purple, dimming into the horizon.

The young woman Henry had called Madison walked through his line of sight, leading, it seemed, two of the other passengers on her raft. Both middle-aged men panted with exertion, their arms full of dry bags, tents, and day packs. Her arms were empty, her hips rocking easily with each step, and she glanced in Brayden's direction. He nodded and she smiled coyly, a conspiracy of some sort, with a hint of provocation, then the three of them passed and he watched them climb a short rise for a place to pitch their tents.

Brayden turned his chair toward the beach and watched as Dylan tossed a horseshoe at the distant stake, hearing the *clang* as it glanced against it. The sound seemed distinctly human out here in the wilds, foreign and brash. Dylan shouted something as Henry spun his own horseshoe toward the goal, landing it with a dull thud in the sand.

"Looks like fun, huh?" The voice startled Brayden, and he twisted to see who had spoken. Madison wore her hair in a loose bun, a bundle of straw held in place with a silver butterfly clamp. Her eyes were pale blue, her skin reddened from the day's sun.

"Yes..."

She smiled a row of teeth as perfect as a pair of dentures, her nose as straight and petite as a fashion model's.

"I heard about your fall out of the raft today."

"Yeah, that was..."

"You're OK now?" She nodded, a prompt for him

to do the same.

"Oh, sure. It was pretty startling though, at the time."

"Oh, dear." She reached as if to place her hand on his and let it hover there.

"Madison!" One of the men that shared her raft was yelling for her. "Where do you want this?" He held up what looked like an unfolded tent.

She gave a quick pout. "Better go see what he needs."

"Right."

She was gone as quickly as she'd arrived, sauntering up a little slope toward the man with the tent in his arms. He watched them pointing here and there, debating where he should pitch her camp. He wondered whether they were friends or had just met on the trip.

"Beautiful campsite, isn't it?" Another young woman nodded a greeting and plopped into the chair Henry had used.

"Yes."

"My name's Em, in case you forgot. Short for Emily." She was a passenger with Madison, on the other raft. Her cheeks were high and tanned, like she'd been hiking in the desert sun before joining the river trip, and her smile was wide and honest, the tiniest gap between her two front teeth. Dark hair angled across her forehead then reached to her shoulders, where it curled just a pinch.

"Brayden," he pointed to himself. "I'm terrible with names, for some reason."

"Me, too. After two names at once, my brain just seems to shut the rest of them out."

"I know."

"What brings you on this trip?" She turned her chair toward him.

"I'm here with my Uncle Henry." He pointed toward the horseshoes. "And Dylan, a work associate of his. Henry won two seats on this trip for some sort of sales competition and asked me to come."

"Sales?"

"Insurance."

"Do you work with your uncle?"

"Temporarily. I mean, for now. I do some writing, with summaries and such, and help them with their reports." He sensed curiosity in her sharp brown eyes, but didn't feel like discussing the office right now, or being reminded of what he'd seen on Henry's computer.

She nodded.

"What brings you on this trip?"

"I just started a new job with a non-profit group. You may have heard of it, Save Our Canyons, SOS. The

SOS is a play on words, meaning it's urgent, of course, but it also means Save Our Selves. It emphasizes our connection with these rare places." Her eyes glistened when she smiled. "We're dedicated to protecting desert canyons all over the American southwest. We raise money and lobby for state and federal laws to keep these places wild and protected." Her head bobbed a bit when she spoke, an excess energy spilling through her words.

"Yeah?"

"And we do public education, provide school materials and workshops and day hikes for kids, that sort of thing. I wanted to see this stretch of the river and get up into some of these remote canyons."

"Sounds like a worthy cause."

"Well, we never have nearly enough money to do what's needed, but, yeah, it's something I really support."

"Do a lot of groups do trips like this, through the whitewater and up into these canyons?" Brayden's finger circled the air.

"I guess you could say there are a lot of them. Enough to need to be very careful about packing out whatever you pack in. It only takes one group to mess it up for everyone else."

"I guess that's true. What about private groups out here?" He waved toward the river.

"They're supposed to follow the regulations, but there's not enough park staff to check on them. Most people are fine, but I've heard that some leave trash and even take artifacts, though it's illegal."

"There are artifacts out here?"

"Used to be all over the place."

The sun dropped below the distant rim, a final flare spread thin along the horizon, torching the bottoms of puffy clouds. Daylight wafted upward into the night, a canvas of fiery marigolds.

They watched together as the heat rotated farther away, the clouds fading to a pasty gray.

"I have no words beautiful enough for this," he pointed.

"Me neither," she sighed.

CHAPTER 12

Ivan wanted an early start, while the air remained cool. They'd arrived at campsite number one late last night, after a stay upriver at Hangman's Canyon. The morning sun cast a warm glow on cliffs across the water, but much of Devil's Tail Canyon was still bathed in shadow. He ate two sticky-sweet granola bars and washed them down with a mug of instant coffee heated on his portable stove. He planned a scouting trip along the northern wall of the canyon then into an area that Barc said held a beautiful little waterfall and pool that dried up later in the season. There were two trails up to the pool, he'd said, along opposite sides of the canyon. From there, you could stand on the rock wall above the deep pool and follow the drainage upstream to another bowl and maybe even to another above that, all the way to the top of the plateau. Up there somewhere, beyond where the tour groups went, he hoped to find virgin ruins with undiscovered artifacts. Though he didn't expect to go too deep into the canyon on this reconnoiter, he had his daypack with him to carry away whatever he could find.

Ivan was anxious to get going and had already decided to let Jeb and Barc sleep as late as they wanted. This would be his own quick trip, and they could all go up later, with the ladder, if his binoculars helped him locate any ruins of interest. Besides, he had to admit that his brush with that ghost of the Pueblo, his near fall from the top of the ladder, still spooked him a little. Maybe more than a little. He did not want to explain that strange episode, or his chagrin about it, to anyone else. He would rather check things out by himself for now, reassure himself that the weird encounter was just a one-time mishap. Maybe he could forget about the whole thing. And just to be safe, if he needed the ladder to get into some ruins, he'd have Jeb or Barc with him next time.

He set out along a narrow path that led away from their riverside camp and up a steep embankment. Beyond, the trail wandered near the northern side of the big canyon. Broken rocks huddled near the sheer rock, which rose nearly three hundred feet into a turquoise sky. Occasionally, he could see a parallel trail on the opposite side of the canyon. He knew that by mid-afternoon, the sandstone cliffs would be baking.

He walked for nearly two miles through open grassland and tight switchbacks when the trail turned sharply to his right. A faint sound of moving water reached his ears and two hundred feet later he stepped out of a jumble of rock and to the edge of a pool of water nearly fifty feet across. He took a moment to look around. A steady drizzle fell from the edge of a cliff forty feet above the pool. Maidenhair ferns clung to the back of the sandstone bowl, just within an intermittent spray. Sandy ground circled the pond, probably packed from the feet of rafters who came here to admire the sight and dip in the refreshing water.

The sun had risen higher on its arc, lighting the narrow canyon and lending the grass an iridescent glow. Ivan searched for a way above the falls and wound through table-sized boulders for a while before he saw a cairn, a man-made stack of stones that showed him the way. He scrambled up a four-foot crack and worked past a slippery rock to a place where the ground leveled out. He walked toward the tiny stream and peered over the edge of the cliff. From above, he could see to the bottom of the pool below, its water a mossy green.

Behind him, the land sloped gently upward toward a ridge that reached from one end of the narrowing drainage to the other, an obstacle that might be hard to overcome. But the ground was remarkably flat where he stood, scoured out by spring run-off or flash floods that tore their way through this country after a thunderstorm. He followed the bubbling creek a while and bent to his knees to take a look. The water shimmered in the sunlight, a gentle current distorting the sand and pebbles on the bottom of the tiny stream. He looked up again at that next ridge and considered how to get on top of it. He couldn't see a trail and would have to search for a way, one step at a time. A little later, he thought... He resolved to stay here for a snack, sat next to the leisurely stream, and set his pack down. When he pulled a granola bar from the side pouch, his pocket knife stuck to the wrapper and flipped out and into the water.

"Damn it." He reached gently into the sandy bottom and pulled out the knife. Several small rocks clung to the closed blade and he began to pick them off, but one gleamed like broken glass and he rolled it in his fingers for a closer look.

"Holy crap!" He held a small diamond, clear and clean, cut as if it had been in an engagement ring. "What are the chances of that?" He wondered whose ring had lost its stone up here, never to be reclaimed by the owner. "Wait till Jeb sees this little bonus!" He smiled and pocketed the stone then stared down into the sand until he thought he saw another diamond, then another, and then something green, rectangular, not a natural shape at all, and his breath seemed to catch on something ragged.

He reached into the cold water and scooped a pile of sand into his palms and rolled through it with his thumbs.

"Holy flying shit."

Among the rough sands were a handful of polished diamonds and an emerald half the width of his fingernail.

CHAPTER 13

No one could search over five hundred square miles of Canyonlands National Park or the adjacent Bears Ears National Monument all by themselves. But anyone trav-elling there – especially anyone cooking moonshine – would have to have regular contact with sources of water and Deputy Dawson had marked all the possible sites on the corkboard in his basement command center.

He'd decided to take four vacation days and raft the Colorado River through a popular whitewater stretch and talk to the river guides he came across. He'd ask them to keep an eye out for the elusive pony-tailed hermit of the canyons and for evidence of illegal moonshining or other shenanigans. He'd hand them his official sheriff's office business card but with his home number scratched over the office contact. He had only one pair of eyes, but could multiply that into dozens if he could convince the professional guides to watch for the unusual.

The National Park Service was in charge of these huge regions, nearly the size of Rhode Island. The sheriff had a mutual aid and cross-deputization agreement with the feds, and they cooperated all the time. Neither the feds nor the county had authorized an investigation. Well, not formally, at least. But Dawson did not plan to ask permission – better to seek forgiveness later, if it came to that. And he'd be on his own time, chasing a couple of cold cases, something other officers had done when there wasn't enough time in the work day to keep pursuing them.

The sheriff's office had limited search and surveillance capability. Even when they knew that someone specific was missing or injured in those deep, twisted canyons or on the massive plateaus, finding them often depended on luck and intuition. It wasn't like in the movies, where they just ordered up a military satellite or high altitude drone or infrared imagery. The office was considering the newest drone technology, but they still required human operators within a limited radius. But Dawson did need one tool from the office, not for finding someone but for survival in case of an accident: an emergency satellite phone. He'd waited until the weekend shift was on duty to check out one of them, when the sheriff would be gone and Dawson's favorite desk clerk would be there.

He pushed past the swinging glass doors and into the lobby.

"Good morning, Natalie."

Her eyes shifted downward and her freckled face blushed lightly. "Evening, Deputy Dawson." She pushed some papers aside.

"Gotta check out a sat phone from supply." His voice sounded deeper than usual, official stuff at hand.

"Sure." She reached under the countertop and slid a clipboard toward him. "Going into some back country?"

"Yeah. Four days. Gonna raft and get into some of the deeper canyons." He took the pen tied to the metal clip and filled out his name and dates for use of the special phone. "Never know when you might find an emergency situation."

"That's Deputy Dawson," she smiled, "always prepared."

"Well…" He stammered a moment and caught himself. Stay cool. Stay on task. "Just good training." He glanced at her sky blue eyes and looked quickly back to the property check-out list. For weeks, he'd been working up his nerve to ask her out…

"Hey, Dawson." Deputy Freeman reached his head around the doorframe of the back office. A giant of a man, outwardly friendly, he still made Dawson just a little nervous.

"Hey." Dawson nodded at him.

"Going into the back country?"

"Yep."

"Looking for sasquatch again?" Freeman's lips curled in a half-smile that straightened at the edges, some part of it an amused sneer.

"No. Of course not." He stiffened.

"Oh, well, OK." Freeman did not believe him.

"Going whitewater rafting." He pointed at the clipboard. "Checking out a satellite phone."

"Right."

"Better safe than sorry."

"Right. Well," he waved and moved back into the inner office, "good hunting."

Dawson watched Freeman leave and released a sigh.

"Don't pay any attention to big shot, there." Natalie scowled.

Her remark surprised him, and he gave her a quick nod.

She spun the clipboard toward her and read his scribble. "OK. We won't see you until later next week, then?"

He put his hands on the countertop and refocused. “Right. I’ll be on my shift as soon as I get back.”

“Well, take good care of that sat phone, and yourself.”

“Will do.” He lifted his left foot to turn, caught it on his pants leg, and stumbled forward. Damn it.

Her eyes crinkled with her smile.

He grimaced, nodded, and walked more or less normally the rest of the way to the supply room.

CHAPTER 14

Brayden woke to the sound of Connor's voice: "Coffee!"

He slipped on a pair of nylon pants, the kind with legs that zipper off into shorts, and a shirt advertised as having built-in sunscreen. He brushed his teeth with water in the lid of his water bottle, combed his hair, and tightened a Cubs baseball cap on his head.

The morning breeze was downright cold – all three guides had long sleeve shirts and George wore a knitted ski hat. Brayden blew into his hands and hurried to the coffee pot. The black liquid steamed in the air, but it felt good sliding down his throat.

Freshly broken eggs hissed as they spread across the sizzling grill, Audrey folded them back on themselves with practiced strokes. "Grab a plate!"

Brayden shuffled in front of the grill, fork and plate in one hand, coffee in the other, and watched as she stirred onions, peppers, and pieces of bacon into the mix.

"It's kind of a work of art, isn't it?" The voice came from behind him.

Brayden turned toward a young man in a flannel shirt, glasses loose across his nose, brown hair still crumpled from sleep.

"I'm Carl."

"Brayden." He touched his mug to his chest.

"I could eat a dozen of these right now."

"Me too." Audrey spread shredded cheese on the eggs, folded them over, and slid them onto their plates.

"Cinnamon rolls down there." She pointed with her spatula.

In Brayden's line of sight was Madison, her hair tied in a bun, walking toward the kitchen. She flashed him an unexpected smile, and he managed a quick nod.

He and Carl found two camp chairs posted next to each other and sat. They ate quickly, while the food was still hot.

"Where are you from?" Brayden wiped his breakfast roll across the plate, gathering the last of his eggs.

"We're from Moose Lake, north of Saint Paul."

"What's your wife's name?"

"Claire. But we're not married. Can't afford it yet." Carl sipped his coffee.

"Can't afford a wedding?"

"Not a nice one. Not and do the travelling we want to do this year. How about you? Where are you from?"

"Chicago. I'm working right now for my uncle, Henry, who must still be sleeping." He glanced around the camp. "He works with Dylan." Brayden aimed his mug toward a man standing at the grill.

Carl nodded. Coffee in hand, he pushed his glasses tighter against his nose. "What do you do for a living?"

"My uncle's in insurance, sales and management. I've been helping in his office with reports, presentations, questions from clients. Temporary gig. You?"

"I'm working on my dissertation in freshwater snails, a DNA study. Claire's planning to teach in elementary school, first or second grade."

"DNA? Cool."

"I'm kind of a snail nerd, but the genetics of their mucous membranes, variances among the species, shows some strange potential."

"Well, it must be great to love what you do."

Carl glanced at him sideways.

"You don't like it?"

"The study of mucous? Really?" He chuckled. "But the economic potential keeps me totally into it."

"Economic?"

"I'm learning to chart, slice, and splice DNA. Can you imagine what that will be worth when we learn how to fully apply that to human medical trials? A cure for diabetes?"

"Wow."

"It'll be a tough market to get into, I know, but I don't plan to live in student housing and eat ramen noodles for the rest of my life, you know."

"Right." Brayden turned toward the river, its subtle, bubbling, rhythm quieting the air. He stared at ripples in the water, motions that feigned a downstream path but kept circling back up to whatever rock or log lay beneath them. Across the water, a flat expanse of sandstone rose straight up, five hundred feet in the sky, gilded in bronze by the rising day. Sunlight rolled across the sandy beach, and he watched as it slid past him and lit their camp, warming his skin.

Clang, clang!

Connor banged a spatula against the coffee pot. "Everyone! Last call for breakfast! Up and at 'em!"

"I'm going for another roll. Want one?" Carl stood.

"No, thanks."

Henry, Claire, and the rest of the late sleepers shuffled toward the grill, and the camp filled with friendly chatter and clanking bowls as they all ate, cleaned their plates, sipped their caffeine.

Audrey seemed to turn the kitchen over to George, who scraped the grill, gathered trash, and began washing dishes. She hopped onto an upside down bucket and raised her hands.

"OK, everyone, let me have your attention for a moment."

Voices lowered and faces turned toward her.

"For all who want to, we're hiking this morning to a beautiful pool of water up the canyon, about two and a half miles each way. If there's enough water in it, we can wade in and cool off. The hike is uphill on a narrow trail, so wear your best boots or shoes. Everyone slather on the sunscreen and fill your water bottles before you leave, it's going to be a scorcher. We'll bring extra granola and snacks for lunch. Now, normally, no one gets hurt on this hike but we have to tell you to be careful. The trail is rough in most places and even if you're tempted, please, please, please do not lean over the edge of any steep cliffs!" Her smile seemed to carry some pain along with it. "Even a steep hillside can carry you way, way down and bang you all up. So place your steps carefully, try not to twist an ankle. It hurts like the devil and it's no fun to have to carry you out and, yes, we had to do that a couple of seasons ago. We have an emergency satellite phone, packed in a small, red dry bag right on top of Connor's raft." She pointed. "Easy to find. If Connor or George or I are incapacitated for any reason, now you know where it's at. I've only ever had to use it once, that year we had the sprained ankle. And though we have it, it still took a day and a half for help to get to us that year, then they had to get him out, so… no one sprain any ankles or fall off any cliffs, please!" She raised her arms and smiled. "To recap…" she raised a finger for each point. "Footwear, sunscreen, water, sat phone, no leaning over cliffs. OK, everyone get ready and we'll leave in twenty minutes."

CHAPTER 15

Ivan searched furiously for more diamonds, digging with his fingernails, filtering water over his palms, cramming tiny stones into his pants pockets when any one of them resembled something that might be a gem. Soon, his pants were wet from the dripping jewels, and he seemed to have exhausted his find. There must be more of them, maybe higher up the drainage, washed here by a spring storm.

He knew the pond below this rim was a popular spot for visiting rafters. There could be a group there before too long, and they might come up to this spot to look around. He needed help.

Ivan stood and noted the sun's position on its arc across the sky. If he hurried, he could get Jeb and Barc here by noon. This trip had been a real bust so far, but these gems would turn it all around, and he was excited to share the good news. He turned and hurried down the trail, past the pool, staying on the narrow path that paralleled the main route used by the tourists. He didn't want to run across any of them. He tried to keep a steady pace over the uneven terrain and, going downhill, made better time than coming up.

In less than an hour, he'd reached open ground above their camp and slowed to catch his breath.

Their tents were pitched on spots of even ground above the river. A separate tent, tall and narrow, was staked over the porta-potty, Ivan's tip of the hat to privacy that Barc had teased him about. Two blue rafts were docked along the bank, one with his lightweight ladder strapped to its frame. Barc was nowhere in sight, but Jeb was seated by the rafts, working a rag over something in his hands.

Ivan wound his way through the grassy area and down to the river.

"Hey," Jeb glanced up and returned to his task.

"Hey, yourself, Jebediah."

Jeb reacted to something different in the tone of Ivan's voice, a barely restrained optimism, and turned back toward him.

"We're going to be rich, Jeb, fuckin rich!" He dug deeply into the pockets of his cargo pants. "Wait till you see what I've found up there!"

Jeb wrapped a 9mm pistol in the oiled rag and slid it under his camp chair.

Ivan stretched his right hand toward Jeb, whose brow rose with curiosity.

"Here."

Jeb opened his palm.

Ivan poured the gems into Jeb's hand, staring intently at their sharp sides and gleaming edges.

"Holy mother." Jeb's eyes rounded into wide, blue orbs.

"Diamonds, dozens of them, mixed into the sand in the little creek up above the pool, maybe two miles back." Ivan nodded up-canyon. He moved his other fist over Jeb's palm and emptied another batch of gems into his hand.

Jeb stood up abruptly, sending his chair backwards to the ground, staring intently at the stones, at Ivan, and back at them. "You just found this, lying around up there?"

"Yes!" Ivan began to bounce on the balls of his feet. "We've got to get back there and find the rest!"

"How the hell?"

"No clue, but they must have washed down with the rain. We need to find the source…"

"Before somebody else does."

"Right-o."

"Get that dry bag for me." Jeb nodded toward the bag on the ground.

Ivan lifted it and held it open as Jeb dumped the jewels into the bag. He brushed his hands to make sure they had all gone in then took it from Ivan and rolled and clipped it shut.

"Where's Barc?"

"Fishing, downriver somewhere. I haven't seen him for a while now."

Ivan called Barclay's name twice, then a third time, but heard no reply. "We need to get back up there."

"Damn it, we'll have to meet up with him later." Jeb clipped the small bag of jewels to his belt and hopped into the closest raft. He rummaged through another pack, pulled out a shoulder holster, and strapped it on.

"Let's go." Ivan shifted his weight from one foot to the next.

"Grab your water and some food." Jeb stepped out of the raft, went to the pistol he'd been cleaning, and slipped it into the holster. "We'll be gone all day."

CHAPTER 16

The trail led the group to an open expanse of grass and sage that rose gently above the river, lifting them to a plain where they could see the massive cliffs across from their camp and a steep side canyon upstream, on the other side of the water. The path turned sharply into a series of steep switchbacks that kept Brayden panting for air, his skin sweating in the rising heat.

After a while, they came to a narrow canyon filled with brush and saplings and boulders. The route twisted through the tight places, forcing him to duck under branches and to scramble up cracks in the rock, and though there was welcome shade along this route, the climb became even steeper and he finally had to stop for a drink of water.

He looked back down the trail, where Uncle Henry, Carl, Claire, and Connor had stopped for a drink too.

He could hear the rest of the group ahead of him, chatting as they went.

Henry put his water bottle away and began moving again, so Brayden turned and pushed forward. The path wound through more small trees then angled to his right, up a dry, open area where the canyon widened. Once atop that rise, he hiked above the tree line and into a boulder field, where the path twisted, turned, and twisted again for another quarter mile. Voices carried to him rather suddenly, then the sound of splashing water. The trail opened to a level, grassy area and around a short bend appeared a pool of water collecting a steady drizzle from a sandstone ledge about forty feet above them.

Audrey kept a watchful eye on the group. Em was in the water up to her waist, making her way to the tiny waterfall. Dylan removed his daypack and waded into the water, pronouncing his arrival with a satisfied "woooo…"

Brayden went to the right side of the pool and set his pack on a rock. He wore a kind of waterproof hiking sandal, so he left them on. He stepped into the water, too, its luxury surprising him. In moments, he was also waist deep, his body cooling quickly.

Em moved under the falling water, drenching her head and hair and Brayden felt compelled to try it, too. He walked closer, felt the sting of water plopping onto his head, and released a "whoop!"

Em turned and smiled, her cheeks high, eyes crinkling along the edges, her joy infectious, and he grinned back at her then closed his eyes and put his face fully into the raining drops, absorbing the wet, the cool, the surprise of it all.

Henry, Carl, and Claire arrived and waded into the pool. Madison dipped her bare toes into the water but kept the rest of herself dry. After a few minutes, the refreshing water began to chill Brayden and he turned and walked out. He went to the rock where he'd left his pack, removed his shirt, and wrung it out. The desert sun was high in the sky and felt good on his skin, and after he dried he put his damp shirt back on and it felt perfect.

Next to his pack, he noticed a small trail that made its way farther to the right of the pool and up a steep, short incline, where it disappeared.

"Going up?" Dylan passed Brayden on the narrow path.

"Later."

Dylan worked his way higher and disappeared above them. Carl wandered on the trail behind him.

Brayden sat in the sand and rested his elbows on his knees, a slight breeze cooling his chest. He reached in his pack and pulled out the steno pad and a pen, jotted words on the page that he might use later, ideas and words about this place that struck him as poetic.

"How about this?" Henry patted him on the shoulder and looked about. "That was a damn hot hike but this," he pointed at the green water, "made it all worthwhile."

"Agreed."

"Where did Dylan go?"

"Up there." He nodded toward the top of the small waterfall. "I think that little trail takes you on top." He pointed to the sandy path.

"Well, I can't let that guy get ahead of me, can I?" Henry gave him a grim smile. "Might be a neat spot up there. Wanna come?"

"Sure. I'll be up in a minute." Brayden reached for his water bottle.

Henry wound his way up the trail and out of sight.

Brayden glanced at the others, some standing under the drizzling waterfall, others sitting on rocks along the side, chatting, pointing to the tall canyon walls, rummaging through their packs. A sound like steady rain, spilling from the tiny creek above, muted their voices, drowning syllables and blurring vowels. He took a long drink of water, replaced the bottle and steno pad in his pack, and stared at the rocky path above him.

Mindful of Audrey's warning about twisted ankles, he took his time winding past rocks along the ribbon of a trail. When he thought he'd lost the path, he noticed a cairn, and continued on. He was soon past the steep part and onto level ground again, backed up against one side of the canyon. The area opened into another small plain of grass and sage that went a mile or so up-canyon, a whole other level segregated from the pool below. He made his way toward the center of the drainage and saw the sparkle of slow-moving water, two feet wide but very shallow, wandering down the canyon and toward the solid sandstone that formed the waterfall.

Henry squatted on his knees next to Dylan, who seemed to be examining the water very closely. Brayden stepped across the open ground and sensed that something was off-base. Dylan lay by the small creek, not moving at all. Brayden hurried to Henry, who seemed to be locked in place, holding Dylan's wrist. He knelt next to his uncle.

"What's going on?"

Henry did not turn toward Brayden, but shook his head and began to shake.

Brayden touched Henry's shoulder. Dylan's face was turned downward and away, the right side of his head raw and bloodied.

Brayden's throat tightened and his nerves began to jump, beads of oil dancing in a sizzling skillet, and he reached next to Henry's hand, feeling Dylan's wrist, searching for a pulse.

CHAPTER 17

Relic lowered himself carefully, reaching, stretching, his toes barely touching the rock beneath him until he slid the rest of the way down. He'd entered Devil's Tail Canyon from the plateau above, scooting down a narrow slot canyon on the southern side of the drainage and working his way toward a little stream that fed a sprinkling waterfall and a nice pool that might have a group of hikers there – it was a popular place to cool off from the heat. He figured that ladder man – the aspiring thief – might search this area for a remote set of ruins higher up the main canyon or up another branch to the north.

Whomp!

The sound carried a brief echo. He strained to hear more, but only a series of muffled noises reached his ears, so he made his way closer to the open plain, toward where the little brook fell over the edge of the cliff, and peered around the boulders. Across the tiny stream lay a weathered piece of cedar the size of a baseball bat, polished by wind and sand and carried here from the mesa above. He leaned farther around the rock.

A man lay prone by the clear water, his face twisted toward Relic, his eyes unblinking.

"Shit," Relic whispered, blowing his words out with the force of a sneeze. He knew, with grim certainty, that the man's journey through this life had ended.

Another man rested on his knees beside the dead man, his hands fumbling with something, and then a younger one hurried to them both and knelt into the sand. Relic moved to another piece of sandstone, closer to the men.

"What's going on?" The younger one reached for the dead man's wrist and a cold stillness fell upon the scene.

No one made a sound for what seemed like a very long time until, finally, the older man broke the spell. "He's gone."

"How? How did this happen, Henry?"

"I found him this way..."

"Did he fall?"

"Maybe. Must have."

"From where? His head's all bloody, hit on something. Could he have tripped and fallen?"

Henry shook his head.

The younger man covered his face with his hands and pulled them down, stretching his cheeks as if to pull them off.

"But look…"

He dropped his arms and stared into Henry's hand.

"What the hell?"

"Diamonds, Brayden!" He put some into Brayden's hand. "Not rough ones, but cut, like they're ready to mount in rings and jewelry and such and look…" Henry scooped his hands into the sand below the gentle flow of the brook and raised them again, water spilling over his palms, his thumb rubbing through it. "They're in the sand…"

"What?"

"They're all mixed in with the sand!"

"Dylan's dead!"

"Yes, yes, they were in his hand! I found them when I checked for a pulse."

"We have to tell Connor and the group."

"Wait a minute, here, Brayden, wait." Henry raised and lowered his palms. "We have to tell the others about Dylan, yes, but not about what he found."

Brayden's face contorted, his question implicit.

"It's finders' keepers, isn't it? Somebody lost these here, abandoned them, actually, and we've been lucky enough to find them."

Brayden shook his head.

"Look at what's in your hand! A couple of thousand dollars, easy. Don't spit on our good fortune – you've got loans to pay! What's happened here is a tragedy, yes, I get that, but in every tragedy there's an opportunity, too. You can find opportunity and then you have to take it to make it!" Henry slid what he had into his pants pocket.

Relic noticed movement on the other side of the drainage, two men with their backs to him, but then they turned, facing the stream. They must have climbed up the parallel trail, but just when Relic thought they were with the same rafters as Henry and Brayden, he realized that one of them was the thief he'd tangled with earlier, the ladder man. They both crept slowly toward the men by the tiny brook, sneaking in plain sight, words between Henry and Brayden becoming more intense and agonized, but when ladder man's companion raised a pistol in the air, Henry finally saw him and leapt upright.

"Hey!"

Brayden put something in his pocket and stood up too.

"Run!" Henry shouted, turned, and began a sprint

toward Relic's hiding place and the trail leading back down to the pool.

Brayden hesitated for one brief second then turned and bolted, arms and knees pumping frantically, picking up speed, drawing even with Henry.

Ladder man and his pal rushed across the clearing, ten yards away and closing fast. Relic stepped deeper into the jumble of boulders.

Henry and the gunman veered to their right, then farther into the broad tangle of rocks.

Brayden turned to his left and into the maze of rocks that concealed Relic.

Ladder man turned left too, away from the path that went down the other side of the canyon, following Brayden. Relic spun and ran but he could hear Brayden closing in behind him.

CHAPTER 18

In an instant, Brayden chose to go slightly left, toward the jumble of desk-size rocks that might give him cover from the men with the gun, his feet pounding the dust, chest leaning into the run. When he reached the first boulder, he swung behind it, searching for the next chunk of stone, and the next. He turned up-canyon and ran for a giant cube of sandstone, spinning behind it and…

Whump!

He'd run into someone head-on, chest to chest, the crash twisting each of them away from the other in a smash of re-directed energy, the other man grunting, stumbling, spinning away. Brayden stopped and stared at him. The man's hair was long and tied in the back, and he wore a thin goatee on his chin. He had a pack strapped to his back.

The man shook his head briefly and stared in return. "Go!" he pointed north, twisting his head back and forth, searching.

Brayden didn't know if he was with the men with the gun or not, but he knew he needed to keep moving. Where the hell was Henry?

The man with the ponytail sprinted forward, spinning and shoving Brayden away, toward a faint trail running north, cross-ways to the main canyon. Brayden didn't resist. His feet found their rhythm on the narrow path, and he dodged rocks and brush and ran until his lungs exhausted and he had to stop for breath. He found a low rock and plopped into the sand behind it, lowering his head, wheezing for air.

After a moment, he rose above the rock and sat.

The man with the ponytail trotted up the main canyon then turned back to watch for those who were chasing him. He stayed in the open, easily visible, until the men reached the end of the field of boulders, where Brayden and the man had collided. Cliffs rose sharply in the backdrop. The long-haired man stood on level ground, maybe thirty-five yards from the other men.

The man with the pistol raised and aimed it forward, but the man with the ponytail stood there another moment, unhurried, before he turned and ran farther up the main part of the canyon. The man with the gun re-holstered it and turned back toward the jumble of rocks. Maybe he was too far away for an accurate shot. The one without a gun followed the man with the ponytail.

Brayden sat there several minutes, watching the long-haired man shrink into the distance, the other man in hot pursuit.

Who is that guy? Why did he tell Brayden to run a different direction? Was he trying to lead the men away? The gunman had turned back toward Dylan's body and the direction Henry had taken – past and away from Brayden – and was soon out of sight.

Brayden stood carefully and looked about. Some distance away, he could see the trickle of stream wind its way to his right, easterly toward where he and Henry had found Dylan. Had the gunman killed Dylan? Or was his death an accident?

Henry had run back toward the rafters lunching at the pool of water. Brayden needed to get back there, but did not want to retrace his steps – a route that would take him directly toward the gunman.

Had the others heard the commotion? Had Henry warned them, gotten them to safety?

The pony-tailed man continued to lead the other one into the distance. Brayden went back to the tiny stream, stepped up to it, and kneeled. He ran his hands through the sand, dry at the edges of the drainage, wet at the center, searching for more gems, and found a small, reddish one that looked like it belonged in someone's ring. What the hell brought it to this little brook? He did not see any other gems so he put the red one in his pocket and turned back, heading farther north and away from the gunman, the long-haired man, and everyone.

There must be another path back down to the pool, he thought, maybe from the other side of the canyon. He continued on for a while then glanced back toward the opposite cliffs, where the man with the ponytail had been, but this time he saw no one.

Where the hell were they?

CHAPTER 19

Henry weaved his way over and through rounded, burnt-red boulders the size of chairs, hopping over some, sliding down others, until he found a patch of sandy ground hemmed in by massive sandstone.

He went to his knees and stared into the dust, panting, listening intently, thinking, wondering how long he could hide. Where was Brayden?

Where did those men come from? What were they doing there?

His fingers were shaking. He tried to slow his breathing.

The men must know about the gems. They'd seen him and Brayden take some of the jewels – that's what they're after, he was sure of it.

He sat in the dirt and leaned back against one of the giant stones. Think, man, think. What do I do if those men find me here? What do I do if they don't?

The sound of boots scraping over rocks reached his little alcove and his muscles tensed.

The man with the pistol appeared around the corner of a boulder, his expression suddenly alight, his gun at the ready. He stepped over a rock and wound his way casually forward, a man in charge of the situation. He stopped about ten feet away and sat facing Henry, crossing his legs and settling into position. He lay his pistol in his lap.

Henry shivered involuntarily.

"Who do we have here? Do you have a name?" The man's tone was firm and level. Sunglasses hid his eyes, which unnerved Henry almost as much as the gun.

"Henry."

"Well, Henry, good to meet you. I need to know what you know about this place."

Henry tried to focus on the man's voice. He took two slow breaths.

"What do I call you?"

"Jeb."

"OK, Jeb, what do you want to know?" Henry tried to sound relaxed, cooperative.

"Empty your pockets, please."

Henry pulled the mixture of gems and sand from

his cargo pants and held them in his hand.

"How many jewels do you have there?"

Henry counted. "Six, I think."

"Not bad. How did you know they were here?"

"I didn't know. I found Dylan. He had these in his hand."

"The dead man is Dylan?"

"Yes."

"Who else knows?"

"My nephew. Did you hurt him?" Henry's voice raised an octave.

"My partner will find him soon enough."

Henry shook his head and stared into the dust. This bastard had them both. He had to think of something drastic.

"Toss over the diamonds."

"Sure. Of course. But…" he looked up at the impassive sunglasses. "Let me suggest something first…"

"I don't have time for games."

"Neither do I and I'll be quick. You're going to want to hear this before you make your next move…"

The man waited, then gave him a quick nod.

CHAPTER 20

Relic resumed a steady trot up the main canyon, the incline slowly becoming steeper and steeper. Devil's Tail Canyon rose nearly one thousand feet from the level of the mighty river and wound for miles into the back country before it finally topped out on the plateau above. Relic could keep up his pace all day, and he knew that ladder man, in particular, gave up with just a little discouragement.

Relic came to a bend in the meadow creek, turned, and slid off his pack. He grabbed a pair of binoculars and searched for his pursuer.

There, a full mile below, ladder man was still walking toward him, bent at the waist, arms swinging from fatigue. The gunman was nowhere to be seen. Maybe he'd turned back toward the dead man or the pool below.

Ladder man stopped and put his hands on his

knees to rest. Perhaps he was debating whether Relic was worth chasing when he could be collecting diamonds on the beach instead. Or maybe he didn't want another encounter like the one a few days ago at the ruins.

Relic straightened his back, swung the binoculars north, toward the steep side canyon that ran there. After a bit, he found the man who had run into him down below. Brayden.

What the hell were those gems doing way out here? He bent to examine the narrow brook and the sand around it but found no diamonds. Who would have brought them into these canyons? And why were they in the little creek, downstream from here?

Then the answer hit him, obvious as soon as he thought of it. The gems were in the creek because the water was washing them down. And he remembered one place, up toward the top of the side canyon, to the north of the main canyon where he sat, that just might present some answers. The side canyon where the nephew was headed.

Ladder man turned away and began to walk back down the drainage. He'd given up. Gunman was nowhere to be found. There were ruins much farther up this part of the canyon, but they were hidden and difficult to reach. Ladder man was lazy and seemed entirely refocused on the diamonds; he was unlikely to search any farther up here for ruins or artifacts.

Relic put his binoculars back into his pack and moved northeast, on an intercept course with Brayden.

CHAPTER 21

Henry pictured a pair of human eyes behind those mirrored sunglasses on the hulk across from him, gun in his lap. If the eyes, at least, were human, he could imagine a way to relate to the creature and keep on talking...

"Here's how I figure it. Those diamonds came from somewhere, and not just in that little trickle of a creek. They must have come from upstream somewhere, washed down during rainstorms. Right?"

Jeb did not move.

"So, the best way to get the most of them, in the least amount of time, is to gather them from here and move upstream as you go. But that takes a lot of time, sorting through all the sand, the water, all of that. The only way to shorten the time is to increase the manpower. That's one side of the equation, so here's the other..."

Henry took a breath.

"The group of people we're with, the whitewater tour group, they are soon going to find Dylan's body up here, on this level of the canyon. When he does not return, or when I don't return for that matter, they will come looking and find, well..." he glanced to the sky, "at least one dead body. That will mean a race to get through the rest of the rapids and downriver and to the sheriff or FBI or whoever. That will mean you don't have much time to gather all the gems or to figure out where they're coming from."

Jeb tilted his head slightly, as if considering Henry's words.

"Now, if you could get the rafters to stay in this canyon for a couple more days and, better yet, get them to help you find the diamonds in this little creek, all you'd have to do is rob them before they leave. You get manpower to increase the collection of gems and a delay in having law enforcement arrive to shut all this down for good."

Jeb's nod was nearly undetectable.

"Now," Henry scooted forward a bit, "all you need for this to work is a partner." He grinned. "I'll tell the group I found Dylan dead, which I did, and gems in his hands. I'll need these..." he pointed at the sand and gems in the palm of his hand, "to prove my point. I'll say he died from a fall, poor guy. Or maybe a heart attack. He wasn't very old but was never in the greatest health."

Jeb peered at Henry from over the top of his sunglasses. Blue. His eyes were blue, Henry noticed, round with wrinkles below like tiny, humorless, smiles.

"What?" Henry asked.

"I figured you killed him." Jeb slid the glasses back against his brow, covering his eyes again.

"I figured *you* killed him." Henry straightened his back.

"So, it must have been an accident..."

"Exactly."

"Go on." Jeb motioned with the palm of his hand.

"So I tell the group that Dylan died from a fall or a heart attack or something but he found all these diamonds, and all that wealth just drove my nephew crazy and now he's exploring up the canyon, I couldn't stop him, trying to find more diamonds. The group has to bury Dylan. We can't bring a body back through those rapids by ourselves – what if he fell out? We need to get help, but we can't leave Brayden, and he's AWOL, high up in the canyon. We have to find him first. I appeal to the group, one by one, that they should each start their own search and gather effort. It could be worth hundreds of thousands of dollars to them. They'll be gathering what you will steal from them once it's all collected."

"And what will your nephew be doing?"

"Running from you, I assume. But he's going in the direction you want to go to find the source. There could be many more of these jewels higher up the canyon. You go to the source, while I keep the rafters occupied and gathering the gems that have washed downstream. We'll keep meticulous track of it all, and we're sitting ducks when you're ready to rob us."

"What's in this for you, do you figure?" Jeb's brow rose above his glasses.

"Only two things. First, of course, my nephew and I get to live. Then, to keep me quiet forever, we get twenty-five percent of your haul."

"Your nephew will know of this deal?"

"No."

"Two percent would be outrageous." Jeb dipped his chin to his chest.

"Twenty. You'll be wealthy men, beyond imagination!"

"How will you keep the rafters from sending someone downriver for help, before we're all done here?"

"That's part of the real value I'll bring to this. I'll find a way. I can disable the rafts if I need to, get the other rafters to support the decision to stay and search for

Brayden while gathering gems."

Jeb leaned forward. "You would need to sit still, right here, for about twenty minutes. Let me and my partner get the hell out of here."

"Of course."

"Three percent is absolute tops."

"Three percent of the number of gems we collect?"

"Yes."

"Done." Henry reached his open hand toward Jeb, who stood, walked casually toward him, and shook it.

CHAPTER 22

The weirdo with the ponytail was a real pain in the ass, but Ivan was not going to waste more time chasing him into the barrens of Devil's Tail. That was the obvious reason, at least, to stop running after the ghost. But the question niggling at the back of his brain, the one that burned like a lit match, was whether the wild man would cripple him this time, if he actually got near the bastard. "Enough," he pushed the thought away, turned, and made his way back toward the jumble of rocks where Jeb had been.

After a bit, he saw Jeb wave his arms at him, pointing a few yards away from the dead body.

Ivan hurried forward and met him.

"Let's stay away from that guy." Jeb pointed at Dylan's corpse. They hopped the little creek and moved back to the side trail they'd come up. From there, they lowered themselves down boulders and crags to the path that ran parallel to the main one used by the rafters. Drifting voices and splashing sounds kept them quiet and cautious for a while, but after the group was a safe distance away, Jeb motioned for Ivan to sit.

"The ass wipe with the ponytail got away from me." Ivan lowered himself onto a flat-topped rock. "Couldn't keep up with the monkey."

"Where did he go?"

"Farther up the main canyon, along the creek."

"The diamonds could be coming from up there, washing down." Jeb sat on the ground. "Where did the other guy go?"

"North, toward a side canyon. I don't think there's a running creek there, just dry drainage."

"So," Jeb scratched his ear, "it's possible the diamonds could be coming from the side canyon, where the young guy is going, but it's more likely down the main one, where the stream runs all year round."

"Damn." Ivan scratched his boot on the ground. "I wish I'd thought of this earlier – checked the map – that stream goes a long way up the canyon. We can't go on a wild goose chase overnight without more water and food. We're going to have to go back to camp again and get more supplies."

"Well, get this, I caught the third guy, the older one, hiding in the boulders."

Ivan's brow rose with his question.

"So I catch this guy cold and guess what he does? He begs for his life and offers us a deal."

"What?"

"Yeah. He promises to go back to the group of rafters and keep them here, in Devil's Tail, so no one can call the police until we leave, then also to have them gather up all the diamonds they can so we can rob 'em on our way out of the canyon."

"Really?" Ivan tucked his chin to his chest then leaned forward. "No shit?"

"No shit. So I thought about it. Then, I asked him what he wanted in return and he said, well, to live, of course, him plus the other guy, who's his nephew, but he also wants three percent of the gems we steal from the rafters."

Ivan sat up straight.

"He works for us now."

"Holy fuck." Ivan's eyes narrowed. "You agreed to give him three percent?"

"Here's what I figure..." he leaned toward Ivan. "The guy wants to live and wants to get rich. All he has to do is delay the group by having them follow their own instinct to gather diamonds into their own pockets. It just might work. It's a cinch those gems are being washed down from higher up. It gives us time to get up-canyon to find the source, to see if we can find the mother lode, then get back down to get out of here, clean as a whistle."

"We'll have to deal with the ponytail guy or the other one, the nephew. We're likely to run into one or both of them up there." Ivan raised a finger.

"Sure. We'll keep our eyes open, but we have a 9mm." He patted his holster. "They have nothing. And on our way out, we rob the group, which has spent a day or two collecting gems."

"How do we know someone won't go for help, the guides or someone else from the rafter's group?"

"I think our new employee is pretty motivated."

"But not all powerful." Ivan shook his head. "We need to tell Barc what's happened, maybe have him stay at camp and make sure no one goes for help while we're way up in these canyons."

"Good idea. Like you say, we'll need to go on down for extra food and water anyway. And maybe a tarp or something to sleep under."

"Right. So, back to the deal with this new employee of ours. You really expect us to pay him three percent?"

"What do you think?"

Ivan grinned. "What about the dead guy?"

"We didn't kill him. Not our problem."

Ivan bumped his fist with Jeb's.

CHAPTER 23

Henry waited twenty minutes or more, counting to one hundred ten times, then paced, then counted again. He wanted to be sure the gunman had plenty of time to leave.

When he'd waited what seemed like an entire era, he slid to the bottom of the narrow trail and turned. He listened intently but heard nothing; no one seemed to be following him. All in all, Jeb turned out to be a real businessman. Though not perfect, Henry could literally live with the deal and still make out like a bandit. If Jeb keeps his part of the bargain. It's a risk, to be sure, but not a bad one considering Jeb could have killed him then and there, dead as Dylan. Funny how fast your fortunes can turn.

He trotted down the trail, dodging rocks and cactus as he went. When he heard voices, he prepared to meet the others and slowed his pace.

"Connor!" Henry stopped a few yards from the group.

"Yes?"

"I need you over here."

Connor trotted closer.

"I don't know how to say these words so I'm just going to blurt it out: Dylan's fallen and been killed!"

"Whoa, Henry, what the hell?" Connor held up his hands.

"Dylan's dead. Up there, above the pool, I found him…"

"Catch your breath."

"He must have fallen and hit his head on some driftwood up there, there's blood on it, and when I checked his pulse…" Henry dropped his head to his chest.

"Shit!" Connor sprinted toward the path to the upper level and disappeared from view.

Henry turned and followed Connor back to the top. When he got there, Connor stood near Dylan, hands on his hips.

"You found him this way?"

"Yes."

"Holy fuck, he's dead."

"I know." Henry looked toward the ground.

"How did this happen?"

"There's a spot of blood on that driftwood there. Dylan looked OK, but he had some serious heart problems."

"He didn't say anything to us about that."

"No, no, he was a really proud guy, and he wanted to come on this trip. He didn't want someone telling him his heart was too fragile, you know."

"Shit."

"Sorry. I didn't even think about it much. I just figured he knew what he was doing, that he wouldn't come unless he was well enough to come. And he was so young, only in his late thirties." Henry moved away from Dylan's body and sat.

Connor lowered himself to the ground near the stream and stared into the wet sand, his face reddened, chest rising and falling erratically. He wiped his cheeks with the back of his hand and moved his gaze into the distance, sitting quietly. After a time, he stood back up and Henry did the same.

"OK, here's what we have to do." Connor began to pace. "I'll take pictures with my phone of the area, the body, that driftwood over there." He pointed to the side. "For the sheriff. Then we need to move him to a safe place and get him covered up."

"We can't leave him there?"

"Coyotes might find him and, anyway, it doesn't seem right to just leave him out in the open like this. And it'll be easier if we move him close to the rocks we need to use to cover him up."

"Oh."

Connor slid a phone from his pocket and began snapping photographs of the driftwood, the creek, the position of Dylan's body. When he was done, he put the phone away and put his hands back on his hips.

"What a holy, moly cluster…" He shook his head.

"I know." Henry stared at his feet, shuffling them from side to side. "Where do we move him?"

"Near the rocks over there." He pointed. "You grab his legs. I'll get his arms."

"Hey, Connor, do we really have to?"

"Yeah, yeah, we should get him moved away from the water, too. We should keep him dry. And not have him contaminate the stream."

Henry hesitated, then nodded.

Connor went to Dylan's arms and lingered a moment. He stepped fully into the little brook to position himself and then he leaned down, looked away from Dylan's face, and grabbed his wrists. When he began to lift, Henry reached for Dylan's feet and pulled them upward. Dylan's head shifted suddenly downward, bobbing with the momentum, heavy and gross. They struggled with the lifeless weight, barely raising his belly off the ground and then stepped, swung Dylan forward, and stepped again and again until they reached a flat spot where the boulders began. They laid him on the ground gently, Dylan's face settling straight into the dust. Connor turned toward the creek and stepped back quickly, brushing his hands on his pants.

Henry dropped his colleague's feet to the ground and looked away, watching Connor's eyes, still heavy with defeat and worry. They stood there for a while, staring at their boots, the canyon rim, the pale sky above, anywhere but at Dylan.

Connor cleared his throat. "Can you stay with the body while I go back to camp?"

"Well…for how long?"

"I've got to alert the other guides, Audrey and George, and get a tarp to wrap him in. Then we'll need to put stones on top to keep any animals away."

"Oh. We can't bury him?"

"Ground's too rocky, and we'll just have to unbury him when we come back with help."

"OK."

"Let's go back down to the pool for a minute and talk to the others. Then you can go back up to stay with

Dylan's body."

They took unusual care, walking slowly down the narrow path and back to the small pond.

When they arrived, Connor took a deep breath, back in command. "Everyone, out of the water!"

Puzzled faces looked at them.

"Dylan's fallen and died." Connor's voice echoed across the canyon.

"What?" Carl stepped into their path.

"Dylan's died," Henry's voice squeaked. "Up there, above the pool, I found him."

"What?" Em walked quickly toward them.

"He hit his head on the ground or some driftwood up there, there's blood on it, and when I checked his pulse…" Henry dropped his head to his chest.

"Oh my god." Claire put her hand to her mouth.

"Henry…" Em moved to him and gently put her arm around his shoulder.

Madison and Claire walked slowly out of the pool, where they'd been cooling their feet.

Henry nodded a "thanks" to Em and looked up at them all. "He had a heart condition, but he was my colleague, my friend." He let his gaze fall back toward the sand.

"We're so sorry," Claire said, touching her hand

to his arm.

"Turns out Dylan had a bad heart and a hard fall, so here's what we have to do." Connor looked at each of them. "I'm going down to camp to get something to wrap him in until we can get some help. Everyone, either follow me down or stay at the pool. Henry will go back up by himself and watch the body until we get back."

Em and Claire nodded.

Connor turned and walked down the trail that led back to camp, quickly moving out of sight.

Henry's muscles tensed. He remembered something at the rafts. He would have to get it before Connor did or a call to the police could ruin it all.

Em stepped back and looked at Henry. "What can we do to help?"

Henry shook his head and thought. He stretched his open palm toward Madison. "He had this in his hand."

She peered into the glistening sand, her eyes round with wonder. "Is that…?"

"Yes." Henry stared at the stones. "Diamonds, rubies, an emerald."

"What?" Em leaned in to look.

"Where did they come from?" Madison pulled her hair to one side but her eyes stayed on the gems. "They all look like they're cut, too, ready to be set into jewelry."

"I think he found them in the stream up there." Henry nodded toward the cliff above the pool where they stood. "His hand was in the water and these were in his hand."

Madison stepped back and stared at the spot where the water dribbled over the rim.

"They must have washed into that little stream." Henry rubbed his thumb through the mixture of sand and jewels. "There must be more of it up there." He could see thoughts of treasures and sugarplums filling Madison's head.

"Hey, Carl." Henry turned toward him. "Would you mind watching Dylan for me? I just can't go back to see him again, I mean, not right now." He looked to his feet.

"You can't do it?"

Henry stared at his shoes and wiped his nose with a finger.

"Uh, well, oh." Carl adjusted his glasses.

Henry looked up at him. "He's just up the trail and to your right, by the boulders there along the cliff. We moved him away from the creek, back into the rocks. Face down. You don't have to touch him or really even look at him, just keep him in view, you know, from a distance."

"Well, maybe. For a little while."

"Thank you."

"All right." Carl stiffened his back and glanced at his girlfriend Claire. "You stay here."

Claire nodded.

"If you find any more gems, let us all know," Henry suggested to Madison. She nodded and, despite Connor's request, began to follow Carl up the trail.

Henry turned and ran toward the camp as fast as he could.

CHAPTER 24

Deputy Dawson was anxious to begin his search for the elusive hermit. He lifted a five-gallon water jug into his inflatable raft, centered it, then tied it to a pair of half-rings connected to the inside of the rubber tubes. He clipped his daypack next to the water on one side and his tent on the other. You had to pack light for these trips – plenty of water, just enough food, one set of clothes, a first aid kit. And his standard issue pistol, deputy's badge, and satellite phone.

He stepped out of the boat and back onto shore. The sun had reached its mid-morning arc, the temperature moving quickly past the seventies. Good weather was forecast for the next few days, though he knew a storm could rise up out of nowhere and blast its way through the canyons.

No one else was putting into the river here today,

which meant that any rafting groups that were on the water were probably a whole day ahead of him. He'd picked out a couple of potential camping spots for the night. Today would be a long one, running several sets of rapids. Of course, he'd stop anywhere he found any other rafters and give them a talk, a speech he'd been practicing in his head.

Dawson visualized the map at his command center, noting several side canyons with perennial streams, creeks that ran in the spring but dried up in the summer. Two canyons had constant-running springs in their higher elevations: Devil's Tail and Donato Gorge. He figured those two were the most likely, along this stretch of the river at least, for a moonshiner to set up a camp. Both would require a hike through rugged country to get to the springs, so he'd packed his hiking boots in a waterproof bag.

He untied the rope holding his raft to the shore and tossed it into the boat. He pushed the raft farther into the river and, when he hopped on, he slid from the edge onto the floor in an awkward flop. He picked himself up as the boat spun into the current and reached, missed, then grabbed the oars and dropped onto the seat. He began to maneuver the craft to the center of the wide, brown river.

CHAPTER 25

Brayden turned back to the north, took a few more steps, and stopped to listen.

No sound, no motion, no breeze filtered through the canyon; the silence stuffed his ears, filled his head with cotton. It was damned eerie, he thought, this much quiet, not even a crow or a grasshopper or a buzzing fly to remind him that he was not alone. Fire-baked rocks radiated like ovens, the ionized air pulsing like a heartbeat, convections moving the heat in waves over his skin.

Loneliness had never really scared him before.

He wondered whether rattle snakes or coyotes or even mountain lions roamed these wild places, hiding on the high ledges ahead of him, waiting in ambush.

He shook his head, searching his memory for a catchy song, anything to fill the void. When he found one, the bouncy tune helped carry him along.

The ground rose and fell in shallow dimples until, a mile or more away, it reached a solid wall of sandstone maybe eight hundred feet high. From there, the cliffs eased to his right and seemed to dip, leading to another, steeper canyon that ran north and east of the main drainage. It might be easier to hide there, along the rocky base of the cliffs, and find some shade. There ought to be a trail back toward the creek where they'd found the diamonds. From there, he knew his way back to camp. And going forward was far better than turning around and running into the man with the ponytail again or, worse yet, the gunman.

He slid his daypack off and reached for his water bottle.

Empty.

He smacked his dry lips together, squeezed a bit of moisture from his mouth, and put the bottle away. This was a drainage, after all, a gulley where water ran when it rained. Maybe there would be water close ahead of him, a little pool like the one the rafting group had waded in down below. Would it be safe to drink?

Brayden began to make his way over the uneven ground, brushing past tufts of grass, avoiding clusters of prickly pear cactus. He kept his head pointed at the ground, careful with his steps, pushing forward. The afternoon sun beat relentlessly on his neck and shoulders, evaporating his sweat even before it darkened his shirt and, eventually, he began to lose track of time.

What had killed Dylan? Had he fallen? Did the gunman or his partner have anything to do with it?

Who was the man he'd run into among the boulders near the trail? The man with the ponytail. Did he have anything to do with Dylan's death? Was he up here searching for the diamonds they'd found? Hopefully, he was still well behind Brayden and up the main canyon, along with the gunman.

He continued to plod onward, one step at a time, staring at the narrow trail ahead of him. After another couple of miles, he came to a steep incline as he entered the mouth of the side canyon. He stopped to search the area. Behind him, he saw nothing but the open ground he'd crossed, no sign of anyone following him. But the area he hoped would let him circle back to the little creek was a dead end.

Damn it. He was sure he could get there, in theory, by crossing to his left, where he should come out on the northern side of the little creek. But a massive wall of sandstone made any further thought of that impossible.

His shadow stretched to his left, the sun slipping toward the horizon, shade in the narrow canyon reaching across most of the drainage. Only the high face of cliffs opposite the western sun were still brightly lit.

He found a level stone and sat on it. His tongue stuck to the roof of his mouth and he peeled it away, all the inner moisture gone. His mouth had dried in the hot breeze, cracking where his upper and lower lips came together, sore and bothersome. He slid his pack onto the ground and turned to keep his face out of the glare of the lowering sun.

Brayden's head began to ache and in minutes it felt like he had a five alarm hangover. He leaned forward, rubbing his temples, lowering his forehead toward his waist. The blood in his lips throbbed, pumping like thick pudding through a straw, a sensation he'd never felt before. He closed his eyes, squeezing them for tear drops that would not emerge.

Though he was no longer walking, his heart beat faster and faster and though he was not the least bit cool, he felt a chill.

His head began to rumble and jostle, a worn-out roller coaster, bearings grinding on axles without enough grease, and he lowered himself into a patch of rice grass and passed out.

CHAPTER 26

Connor stopped and turned at the sound of footsteps behind him. "Henry?"

"Yes." Henry slowed to a walk and waved.

"You were going to stay with the body…"

Henry slid to a halt. They'd gone nearly all the way back to camp, the tents now visible along the coffee and cream-colored river.

"I just couldn't." Henry glanced at his hands. "But Carl volunteered." He donned a hopeful expression and looked up at Connor. "He offered to watch over Dylan."

"Right, well..." Connor glanced toward the camp. "Let's go get this over with."

Henry nodded and walked behind Connor as they entered a level, grassy area and moved toward the boats.

"Audrey! George!"

Henry stayed close to Connor.

The guides stirred from their rafts and hopped ashore.

"Over here."

They all walked to the camp kitchen and a portable table they'd set up next to the propane stove.

"Where's everyone else?" Audrey tucked her hair behind her ears.

"Gather round." Connor's voice was somber. He explained that Dylan had gone up the trail to the little creek above the pool; that Henry and Brayden decided to follow him up; and when they got there, they found Dylan dead.

"Oh, dear god!" Audrey held her hands to her chest.

"No..." George stepped back.

Connor clasped his hands in front of him.

"How?" George asked.

"He'd had a bad heart." Henry emptied his gaze toward the serving table.

"Oh, that's terrible." Audrey looked to the tops of the surrounding cliffs, her eyes restless, troubled.

"Shit." George stomped his feet.

"That's not all..." Connor put his hands on his hips. "Show them what you found up there."

Henry stepped to the table and pulled sand and stones from his pocket, piling them on the flat surface.

"These were in Dylan's hand when he died. These are what Brayden went further up to find…"

"So, is Brayden back with the group?" Audrey asked.

"No."

"So, we have a dead guest and a missing guest?"

Connor closed his eyes and nodded.

Henry spread the small, rough objects across the table. Audrey and George leaned toward them and abruptly inhaled.

"Look closely, but excuse me, sorry. I really, really have to take a leak…" Henry hurried away and along the sandy shore. When he reached Connor's raft, he waded into the shallow water, feeling the hard rubber with his right hand until he reached the rear of the boat, where the river rose to his knees. He glanced back at them, all huddled over the table, mumbling, lifting jewels one at a time and staring at them. Henry found the small, red dry bag clipped to the frame and quickly reached for it. He unlatched it and pulled it to his stomach, out of view from the guides. He glanced again in their direction.

"How…"

"Call for help…others?"

"…group calm…"

"The tarp…"

Henry observed them carefully as he released the waterproof bag with the satellite phone inside. A moment later, he glanced back toward the river as it floated farther into the glistening ripples and disappeared.

CHAPTER 27

Ivan and Jeb kept a steady pace back to their camp along the river, sticking to the northern trail even though it was rougher than the southern one. They did not want to risk using the same path the rafting group had been on.

"Barclay!" Ivan cupped his hands to his mouth.

Jeb began rummaging through his equipment, gathering what they needed. He grabbed granola, an apple, a small flashlight, and matches.

"Hey!" Barc appeared a few yards away, carrying his fishing pole.

"Get over here!" Ivan waved.

Barc trotted toward the other men. "Where'd you guys go?"

Jeb pointed up the canyon.

Ivan pulled a fist full of gems from his pocket and held them toward Barc. "Guess what the hell we found..."

Ivan told Barc about the diamonds he'd found in the little stream; that he'd run back down to camp but they couldn't find Barc; and that he and Jeb went back up without him. Ivan explained how they'd found Henry and a dead body where the jewels had been and ran them off. "It's our claim, we found it first." Ivan clenched his fist.

Barc released a string of questions.

"We don't know where the jewels came from," Jeb explained, "but it must be upstream, washed down by the little creek. So we're going back up again, with food and water for a couple of days. We're going to follow the stream up the main canyon, camp along the way. As long as we keep finding diamonds, we'll keep following them up."

"I'll get my pack." Barc started to turn towards his tent.

"No, Barc, we need you here." Ivan looked at Jeb. "Tell him."

Jeb explained the deal he'd made with Henry. "But we can't trust him, or someone else in the group, not to leave to get help, like the sheriff or the feds."

"We need a couple more days to see if we can find the mother lode. When we get back, we rob the rafters. They'll have been gathering diamonds near the pool, the little waterfall up there. That will save us a lot of time and work..."

Barc's lips rose in a wicked grin. "So, my job is to make sure the rafters don't go for help and we all rob 'em when you get back, then take off. Strand them here."

"Exactly. But if this Henry dude sees you, or wants to talk to you, be cooperative. Respectful, even. We don't want him to see a double-cross coming before it's too late." Jeb described what Henry looked like.

"The rafter's camp is about a mile from here, so if I'm gonna keep tabs on 'em, I'm gonna have to move my gear a little more down river."

"Keep it hidden. Maybe just use your sleeping bag, no tent. Find a big rock to hide behind. And no cooking." Ivan wagged a finger at him.

"Oh, yeah. We got plenty of cold crap to eat. You want me to watch their camp or follow them up the canyon when they go?"

"Stay down here. We'll be above them and will keep an eye out for them when they're up-canyon."

"Got it." Barc rubbed his forehead. "Any thoughts on how to keep those rafters here?"

"Well," Jeb stood up from his gear, "be creative, but don't confront them. They outnumber you. Keep in mind what we want here: a simple robbery and a quick escape. Try to stay out of sight as long as you can."

"We're really counting on you, Barc." Ivan looked him in the eye.

"Of course."

"And you're going to need my spare pistol." Jeb reached into one of his bags, pulled out a snub-nose .38 special and a packet of extra bullets, and handed them to Barc. Then he reached under his seat and pulled out a round, green object.

"Let's get going." Ivan fidgeted by the shore.

"Heads up!" Jeb tossed the round thing to Ivan.

Ivan caught the grenade and stepped suddenly backward, cursing Jeb, cradling the explosive device like a fragile Christmas ornament.

CHAPTER 28

Hands in his pockets, Henry meandered along the sandy shore toward the guides.

"I'll go back up and secure Dylan's body." Connor stared up the canyon.

"I want to help. He was my friend." Henry looked them in the eye.

"Are you sure you're up for it?"

"Yeah. I just needed to get away from him for a while. But I know I have to go back and face it. I have to face the fact that he's dead. And we need to at least give him some kind of respectful burial, even if it's only temporary."

"All right." Connor rolled a blue tarp tightly and tucked it under his right arm. "Audrey and George will stay here and call for help and get the camp ready for the group to return. We'll stay here another night, of course, and wait for help."

Henry nodded. "Ready when you are."

The guides shared a somber glance, and Connor turned toward the trail at a steady walk. Henry followed quietly behind.

It took them nearly an hour to climb the twisting trail upward toward the tiny waterfall and the pool beneath. As they grew near, scattered voices echoed against the canyon walls.

Everyone stopped talking when Connor and Henry appeared at the pool. They continued quietly past the group, climbed through the steep part of the trail, and made their way toward the body.

Carl stood quickly from a spot just off the trail. "Hey, glad you're back."

Henry shuffled towards him, hand outstretched. "Thank you so much for looking after Dylan. We appreciate your generosity in this terrible time." Henry shook Carl's hand, guiding him gently back down the path to the others. "Really, really appreciate you pitching in like this."

"Sure." Carl glanced at Connor then slid his hand from Henry's and moved steadily toward the wading pool below.

Connor spread the tarp on the ground next to

Dylan. Together, they lifted him onto the tough plastic and set him down. Connor covered the body with part of the tarp, then, together, they rolled it into a tight cocoon. Neither said a word. Then Connor began placing stones along the side of the body, setting a foundation, of sorts. They continued adding layers of rocks until the tarp was fully covered, only a few pieces of it visible here and there. When they were done, they both faced the make-shift grave and hung their heads. Henry could hear Connor mumble a short prayer. He added his "amen" to Connor's.

Henry followed Connor back down the steep trail and into the flat, open area surrounding the natural pool. He took a deep breath and kept his eyes on the ground, though he knew the others were looking at him, wondering how he was handling the death of a colleague, wondering how they would feel if it had happened to them.

The sun had begun to lean hard toward the distant mesa, shadows spreading deeper into the canyon.

"Time to get moving," Connor announced. "Night comes quickly here, and we need to be off the trail before then."

"What about Brayden?" Henry hooked a thumb on his belt.

Em and Madison glanced at them, listening in.

Carl and Claire stepped closer to the group.

Connor stepped toward the little waterfall and bellowed Brayden's name again and again, the sound bouncing off the cliffs.

No one answered.

"Henry," Connor turned toward him, "Brayden's got his pack with him, right?"

"Yes."

"And he left of his own accord."

"Yes." Henry blinked.

"So he has water and snacks with him for whatever hike he's taken. Whatever caused him to leave us, we have to believe he's all right. He made a decision to leave and he'll have to decide to return. Brayden can spend the night out here or hike on down to join us for a late supper, but we can't just hang around waiting for him to decide what he wants to do. We have to look out for everyone else."

"But what if he's hurt?" Em stepped forward.

"We can't find him in the dark, let alone help him. We can't endanger anyone else like that. We'll just have to try at next light."

Em dragged her toe through the sand and looked away.

Henry knew to keep the secret of the gunman

and his accomplice. He looked at the ground and gave a short nod.

"So, everyone, follow the trail back to camp. I'll take up the rear; no more stragglers."

CHAPTER 29

At first, Brayden thought it a delusion, the gentle touch of cool water on his lips, dribbling, spilling off his face. But the sensation persisted, and something told him he should slurp it all in and roll it around his parched tongue, so he did.

"That's good."

The voice was vaguely familiar and not unwelcome. Brayden held a quarter cup of the precious fluid in his mouth, wishing it would soak up like a sponge, then let some of it run down his throat, rough as sandpaper, and he nearly coughed. More dripped in, and he kept swishing then swallowing it, catching his breath in between.

"Can you hold this?"

Brayden nodded, his eyes still mostly closed, achy and dry. He reached until he found the bottle and held it up to his lips, pouring more quickly now.

"Not too fast. Take your time."

He stopped for another breath and repeated the process.

"I thought maybe I'd lost you..." The man sat back on his knees. His chin wore a thin goatee, his black hair pulled tightly into a ponytail. His skin stretched like tanned parchment over wiry muscles, eyes black holes that sucked in the light around them. He was the man Brayden had smacked into back near the creek, when they were running somewhere through the jumble of boulders, both in a mighty hurry.

What is he doing way out here?

Brayden took another swallow, and the water began to slide down more easily.

"Just keep a steady drink going every minute or so. Drink the whole bottle." The man pulled a bladder of water from a large daypack and drank from the tube attached.

Brayden sat up against a rock, and the motion made his head throb. The man pulled three aspirins from a bottle and offered them. Brayden quickly washed them down.

The sun had nearly set, its warm glow rising into purple sky, lifting the oppressive heat. The ground was all in shadow now, here and up the narrow canyon. The man had made a small ring of rocks and filled it with grass and twigs. Dry branches were stacked against another rock some distance away, firewood for the night.

"Drink like a fish." The man motioned toward the water.

Brayden nodded and took another sip.

"We humans are mostly water, you know, about sixty percent."

"Yeah," Brayden croaked.

"About the same for the whole planet – over sixty percent covered in precious water. We cycle it through us all the time, just like the planet, it's what we're made of; we're in a relationship with it. We need to treat it right. Respect it."

"Yes." Brayden stared at his dusty shoes, feeling his heart contract, release, contract, release. He thought about the river that had tossed him from the raft and could have drowned him, too much of it all at once, and the water this stranger had given him, the moisture that brought his tongue and throat and heart back from the edge of a dry, grinding, death.

"So how's your relationship with water going?"

"Getting better, I guess," Brayden raised the bottle in a quick gesture.

The man bobbed his head, unknowable thoughts

rambling behind his eyes.

"Who are you?"

"Name's Relic."

"Relic?" Must be a nickname, Brayden thought. But who is he, really? And what does he want? Brayden took a longer swallow, the water cooling his belly.

"Yep, just Relic." He set the bladder of water aside. "You're Brayden, right?" He reached for a nearby rock and set it between his legs. He pulled a hunting knife from a sheath on his belt and examined it closely, rubbing his thumb alongside the edge.

"How did you know?"

He began to pull the blade carefully across the stone, the heavy scrape of it some sort of rough premonition. "Heard you and Henry talking, before the guy with the pistol and the ladder man—"

"Ladder man?"

"...showed up. I ran into that guy in the canyon upriver from here. He's a thief. He's looking for old Pueblo ruins to see what he can steal. Has a ladder with him."

"Really?"

Relic nodded.

"So, what's the ladder for?"

"To reach the high sites. The old Pueblo people built some of their best homes and lookout posts high up in the cliffs. They got up there with steps carved into the sandstone or with wooden ladders so they could defend them and keep them safe from thieves. Some of the lower sites have been looted, over the years. I guess this fella figures a ladder will get him to places where he can still find some treasures."

"That's a federal crime, isn't it?"

"Yep. So when those two went after you and Henry, all three of us started running. Henry went one direction and you and me, well, I guess we circled into each other in the rush of it all. Then you went north, through the open ground, toward this side canyon." Relic pointed behind him. "I went west, along the general direction of the little creek, 'till the ladder man petered out and gave up."

"Wow. Yeah, we just about took each other out of the race." Brayden took another drink then set the bottle on the ground. "Hey, did you lead that guy away on purpose, the ladder man? To keep him away from me?"

"Yep."

"Hey, thank you. Then you came this way and found me here?"

"Yep." Relic continued to hone his blade, an edge that Brayden thought looked plenty sharp enough already. "So what's your story?"

"I'm here with my Uncle Henry on a whitewater

rafting trip."

"But somebody died up here, and two men with bad intent were chasing us. What the hell is all of this about?"

Brayden swallowed. "The group went to a pond, of sorts, below there. Dylan works with my uncle. I work in the same office, but just doing some low level stuff for a while…" Henry's computer screen, filled with columns of dates and entries, flashed into his mind. "I just graduated. My degree is in English. I do some writing, reports and summaries, that sort of thing, for Dylan and others in the company. Anyway," he shifted forward, "Dylan went up from the pond, to the top of the little waterfall. Henry followed him and I followed Henry, just to see what was up there. Henry found Dylan dead, with a handful of diamonds in his fist."

"Diamonds?"

"Yeah, half a dozen in that little creek."

Columns of sunshine rose like spotlights into the air above the western rim, an inferno glancing off the atmosphere. Puffy clouds blushed a couple thousand feet above them and Brayden stared at the iridescence until he noticed Relic staring, too.

"Nothing more serene than a sunset. Except maybe a sunrise." Relic turned back toward him. "That's all you saw at the little creek?"

"Yeah, that's it. We looked up when the man with the pistol was coming at us. He had the gun in his hand, aimed up in the air, but he came toward us like he was ready to shoot us. Henry jumped up and started to run, so I did, too."

"Did the gunman go after your uncle?"

"Oh, shit, I don't know." Brayden's eyes widened.

"I don't know, either. I didn't see the gunman again."

"He could have hurt Henry or even the rest of the group, down by the pond."

"Possibly," Relic checked his knife. "And that's all you saw at the creek?"

"Yeah. Hey, did you hear any gunshots?"

"No."

"Me neither, so I guess that's good."

"Right."

"Wait. Why did you ask me again if that's all I saw at the creek?"

CHAPTER 30

Em finished her salad and salmon, but the food fit for service in any fine restaurant was tasteless tonight, a meal of salted cardboard, a rote process to deliver calories to her body. The death of Dylan had shaken and soured it all, and she was anxious to know what the group would do tomorrow. She dropped her plate into a tub for washing and wiped it clean, dipped it into a rinse, and left it to dry. A group seemed to be forming on the beach, near an unlit campfire. Henry seemed to be speaking intently with Madison, Claire, and Carl. She carried her folding chair to the others and sat to listen.

"That settles it for me." Madison flipped her hair over her shoulder. "I'm going back up to the pool with Henry tomorrow to see if Brayden has come back."

Henry wore a satisfied grin.

"We can't just abandon him. The more of us up

there to help, the more likely we can find him," she added.

"That makes a lot of sense." Carl pushed his glasses higher on his face.

Henry tightened his lips and turned to Em. "Have you heard? Connor said they lost the satellite phone, probably in one of the rapids."

"No…"

"Which is all the more reason to get back up there and try to find Brayden ourselves." He waved a finger. "We're on our own here, we have to depend on each other and stick together."

"No satellite phone?" Em asked.

"Nope."

"What about those diamonds?" Claire cupped her hands on her knees. "We don't know why they're here, where they came from, who they belong to. We should leave them alone."

"What?" Carl sat up straight. "Hell, Claire, it's finders keepers out here. Whoever left them is long gone, that's for sure."

"We should not be going back up there tomorrow to search for more gems," she scolded.

"Babe, we're going back up to find Brayden. If we find a few more diamonds along the way, so what?" Carl smirked.

Claire crossed her arms.

Carl stopped smiling and leaned toward her. "Honey, really, this is a huge break for us. A few more of these gems and we can take that trip to Italy you've been talking about."

"Or have a nice wedding?" Claire's voice rose an octave.

"Of course, babe."

"This is one of those lucky circumstances where one goal is not opposite from the other." Henry held his hands apart, gripping some imaginary ball. "The primary purpose, at all times, is to find Brayden. But if some of you find some more diamonds along the way, it's fine by me. You have to take it to make it, you know. Why shouldn't you be rewarded a little for helping me and my nephew? I really, really appreciate your help with this."

Madison reached her fingers to Henry's. "We'll find him."

Henry said a quiet "thank you" and patted her hand.

"I'm not crazy about going back up where Dylan's body is, either." Claire wrinkled her nose.

"You should stay by the pool, then," Henry said. "But checking the body is another reason we need to go back up."

"And since we're talking about it," Carl looked at

each of them, "what's the alternative anyway? We could sit around the camp all day, but what's the point in that?"

Henry scratched the side of his head. "Em, what do you think?"

"Now that the sat phone is gone, someone should raft out of here for help."

"That's the plan." Connor approached the group and knelt by a metal pan used to hold the campfire, to keep the ashes in place and the sand from being scorched. "George is going out in his raft first thing in the morning. I'm letting everyone know. And anyone who wants to go out with him is welcome to join him. If more people want to leave than can fit on George's raft, Audrey can take more in hers. If not, Audrey will stay here. No matter what, I will stay here to see what we might do to help find Brayden. We'll head back up the canyon right after breakfast tomorrow."

"Sounds good." Henry looked at each of them, watching for agreement. "Em?"

"I'm happy to help find Brayden, so long as George, and anyone else, is going for help. Thanks, Connor."

"Of course."

Henry leaned toward Madison and spoke just to her. "Will you help me convince the others in our group, too? We need as many as we can get to help find Brayden."

Madison nodded.

The sun had dropped below the distant rim, melting shadows into dusk, muting vivid colors of the day into shades of black and white. Connor pulled matches from his pocket and began to light the fire.

Henry sat upright and looked around the little camp. "Excuse me, everyone. Nature calls." He stood and walked upriver along the beach, hands in his pockets, shoulders hunched. The others began to talk about the gems again, how many each had found, whether they were large, small, clear, or colored.

Em wandered away from them.

Henry glanced back at them and then cut a hard right toward a set of boulders at the edge of a grassy flat. There, atop one of the rocks, sat someone Em did not recognize.

She turned for a better view. The silhouette seemed to wear binoculars around the neck and, from a brief movement, seemed to be a man. He quickly disappeared behind the rock he'd been sitting on. Henry walked toward the same spot and then out of sight as well, all of it occurring in just moments. She looked about quickly, but no one else had noticed. A chill shivered through her fingers.

The man Henry had gone to meet was not part of

the group. And he'd been watching them.

CHAPTER 31

"Just checking." Relic slid his hunting knife into its sheath.

"Did you see something else at the creek? Something I didn't see?"

Relic turned his gaze toward the unlit fire. "Not sure. Something I heard, but I couldn't place it. Was Henry the only one who followed Dylan to the top of the waterfall? Before you got there?"

"I think so. I remember Carl and maybe someone else walking around behind me, in the area where the trail goes to the top, but it's pretty steep. I didn't see him or anyone else go up there"

"Got it." Relic nodded.

Brayden shifted his legs and a raw nerve shot through his head. He wanted to ask more, but his brain was still too fragile and he didn't know this stranger at all or whether he really had anything else to tell anyway. He stared into the distance, thoughts spinning through his head, vision blurred around the edges. Had Dylan fallen and hit his head? Had the gunman and ladder man killed him? Could he really be dead? But of course he is. Are those men after just the diamonds, or him and Relic, too? And that computer screen in Henry's office with dates, dollars, and entries that were off-base… Silence stretched into the dusk, his mood morose, gloom weighing on him like a coat of wet mortar. He sat for what felt like an eternity, a mournful soul, then hung his head to his chest.

"God, this is terrible. Dylan killed. Men with guns following us. The whole rafting group in danger and they may not even know it yet."

Relic waited and Brayden realized he had more to tell. "Plus, when I was in Henry's office the other day, I found something on his computer. I found a bunch of payment records I shouldn't have seen and I'm not sure what they mean but there's something odd about them, something off-base… This is all just so impossible."

Relic unstrapped a fleece blanket from the bottom of his pack. "If we stay nimble, options may present themselves."

"How the hell do we do that?" He heard some petulance in his own voice and regretted it.

"We keep our sense of humor. But first, finish that water bottle then go see if you can pee."

Brayden nodded gently and downed the rest of it in a long, gluttonous gulp. He stood carefully, his balance a bit out of whack, and walked into the growing dark.

When he returned, he lowered himself to the ground, panting a little from the mild exertion.

"Here, keep going." Relic handed him the bottle, refilled to the top.

"Thanks." Brayden drank again.

"Pee OK?"

"Kind of a personal question, isn't it?"

"Hurt a little?"

"Yeah, a little."

Relic nodded. "You're pretty dehydrated there, Brayden. Much longer and your kidneys might have shut down on you. You've gotta keep drinking through the night, whenever you're awake." He patted the bladder next to him. "I've got more, so let's get you back in shape."

"I forgot to thank you."

"No, you did that already."

"Oh, well, thank you again."

"Humpf."

Brayden leaned against a rock across from the unlit fire and settled in, feeling a fresh measure of comfort, his headache, for now at least, in retreat. He reached into his pack, pulled out both of his granola bars, and tossed one to Relic.

"Thanks."

They munched quietly for a while, watching the approach of night, then Brayden cleared his throat. "So, are you a hiker?"

"Sometimes."

"Where are you headed?"

"No place in particular. A good traveler is not intent on arriving."

"Oh. Well, do you live out here?"

"Yep."

"By yourself?"

"Sure."

"Can I ask you? Why do you live alone?"

"Kind of a personal question, isn't it?"

"Well, at least I didn't ask you about your pee."

Relic's lips lifted at the edges. "So there's a sense of humor in there after all…" he waved at Brayden "… somewhere."

"Hmm."

Relic pulled a pack of wooden matches from his pocket. With a twist off his tooth, he lit one and held it under the grass beneath the firewood. They both watched it flare into the twigs and begin to take hold.

"Why live alone?" Relic repeated Brayden's question. "You could say it's a matter of volume, really. How much noise can a guy take?"

Brayden squinted.

"You know, noise." Relic waved his hand in the air. "Big egos who think big egos are the peak of achievement. Too many consumers with too much mindless chatter; the volume gets to be too much for me."

"Huh." Brayden thought about it for a moment. "I don't think I could live out here all the time. I mean, do you even get a chance for a hot shower?"

"Seldom a hot one, but I do have a hard rule about showers." Relic held up a finger and waited a beat. "Twice a year; whether I need it or not."

Brayden watched the desert recluse, wondering if he was serious.

Relic tilted his head and smiled a row of pearl-white teeth, his eyes crinkled at the edges.

Brayden chuckled tentatively, still unsure whether a semi-annual bath was fact or fiction, wondering how a canyon hermit could ever get completely clean. "Well, how do you travel with so little?" He waved his palm toward Relic's pack.

"If I can drink with my hands, I don't need a cup.

If I can curl up with a poncho under the cliffs, I don't need a tent."

"So, material possessions are bad?" Brayden tilted his head.

"Shit, man, you think I'm some kind of hippie?" He sounded a little wounded.

"No." Brayden shook his head. Well...

"There's a big difference between need and greed. There's more than enough to meet the need, but never enough to meet the greed."

Brayden looked at him.

"That's from Gandhi." Relic smiled. "Smart man. I'm just doing my part, living with what I need."

Brayden shook his head. Who is this non-hippie, he wondered, this wandering soul, his cheeks stark in the flickering light, eyes deep as the earth's core? "I don't think I could live with so little."

"Wealth has its demands as well as its rewards. Property owns you as much as you own it. The more you have, the more you have to take care of it, the more you're attached to it. Hell, I started out with nothing and I'm proud to say, I still have most of it."

Brayden smiled and pondered the idea. "What if it's really easy, though? If a pile of money just falls into your lap?"

"The diamonds?"

"The diamonds…"

CHAPTER 32

Barc watched as the man Jeb and Ivan had described to him moved away from the rafter's camp and toward Barc's perch. He let the binoculars dangle from his neck and slid off the boulder and out of sight. It took the man a few minutes to reach him.

"Henry?" Barc did not offer a handshake.

"Yes. You?" Henry seemed nervous, a little out of breath.

"A friend. According to a mutual friend…" Barc crossed his arms.

"Yes, good, yes."

"How are things going? Should you risk leaving the camp like this?"

"I needed to update you on a couple of things." Henry stretched his neck from side to side.

"Right."

"Hey, I've managed to convince everyone in the group to go back up to the little pool again and collect more diamonds..."

Barc relaxed his arms.

"...so that part of the deal is all set. We should have a lot more time to collect tomorrow – all day, really – and we should make a pretty good haul."

Barc couldn't help but smile, just a little bit.

"Of course, some of us will wander around and call out to my nephew, Brayden, so you may see us doing that, too. I had to convince some people to go with us to help find him." Henry nodded like what he'd said was the pinnacle of logic.

"OK."

"Also, I got rid of the satellite phone, just like I said I would."

Barc nodded.

"It wasn't easy, either, doing that right in front of everyone, and getting away with it, not easy at all." He shook his finger.

"OK."

"So, it's all been a huge success so far. We're all set up for a big score here."

Barc nodded. "But...?"

"Well, yes… but, there's some talk that George, one of the guides, might go down river tomorrow to get help."

"What?"

Henry raised his palms. "I have a solution, an easy one, see, I've thought all this through. There's more than one way to keep them from going for help too soon like this. We could deflate the rafts, but that would be hard to do without getting caught, and they might be able to patch them up. Or maybe there are other ways, too, but the easiest would be to take their oars and hide them away."

Barc squinted at the man.

"See, without their oars, they wouldn't dare go downriver through the rapids. Each one is tied loosely to the frame with some lightweight cotton rope – see, I've figured this all out – so all we have to do is cut those, then slip the oars off the rafts, hide them in your camp or maybe downstream a bit. Voila," Henry held his arms wide, "problem solved."

Barc crossed his arms again and considered the idea. "You can do this?"

Henry's face displayed defeat. "No. I don't think I can get away with something like that again. Too many people watching me. But I've got everything else all lined up, just like we agreed. I'm thinking it would be best if *you* slipped into our camp at night and took them. If someone hears or sees you, you can run off, no harm done. If I do it, and someone sees me, they'll catch me for sure and then no one will want to go up to the pool again and gather diamonds. If I get caught, they won't trust me anymore, they won't listen to me anymore. The whole plan would fail if that happened and neither of us would benefit. We have to take this opportunity and maximize it; we have to take it to make it. All we need now is a little help from you on hiding the oars, and we'll all be so, so much richer for it! And the risk is lower if *you* hide the oars because if you are seen, you just run away."

This man could sell snowballs in the Arctic, Barc thought with a grin.

"I've taken big risks here, so far. We just need a little help from you, to hide the oars, and we're safe for as long as we need, to gather all the diamonds we can for you guys."

"And for you."

"And for me, just a little cut in the action is all, only three percent. And I'm assembling a whole team of jewel collectors for us both! If you guys tried to find all the diamonds all by yourself, it would take days, even weeks, and you'd be caught by then for sure."

"I get it." Barc held up his hands, a gesture for Henry to stop talking.

Henry put his hands on his hips and glanced back toward the rafter's camp.

"I'll take care of it." Barc pulled his cap more tightly onto his head.

Henry's shoulders relaxed. "Great, great, thanks! I better get back." He turned and scurried across the grassy plain.

The idea of taking and hiding the oars wasn't half bad, Barc thought. Exactly half, in fact.

CHAPTER 33

Relic blew gently on the fire, pushing its flames against the circle of rock around it, scurrying dusk off to bed like an errant child. Brayden watched as Relic combed his hair with his fingers, loosening it, fanning it over his shoulders, Hercules grooming for the evening. Or Crazy Horse.

"Wealth without work leads to injustice and violence. That's another thing Gandhi said. Diamonds can fall into your lap, but don't let them own you, or control you, any more than you are willing. It's not as easy as it sounds. When people start to rationalize, that's when they're in trouble. Remember the difference between need and greed."

Nightfall surrounded them like a breathing cave, its edges shrinking and expanding with the swells of firelight.

Relic pulled a plastic flask from his pack and sat back.

"Is that what I think it is?" Brayden leaned forward.

"My own brew. You're welcome to some, but you have to take a big drink of water too. Liquor will dehydrate you, so you have to compensate. A little gin, a lot of water afterwards. OK?"

"Sure."

Relic handed him the flask.

"Your own brew?"

"Make it at my still."

"You have a still up here?"

"Not in Devil's Tail. A few miles from here."

Brayden poured a swallow down his throat and groaned in surprise at the bite of it. He reached for his water bottle and drank heavily, washing the sting down his gullet.

Relic took a quick drink and handed it back to Brayden, who took another swig, barely got it down, and coughed.

"Thanks," Brayden said, still a little breathless. His belly began to warm, and he shifted his legs to a more comfortable position. He watched the little fire for a moment and took another drink of water. "It feels like we're just running along in the dark…" Brayden rubbed his fingers through the dust.

"We're all just running along in the dark. You have to feel your way as you go, that's just how it is. But look up, now, look at the stars." Relic pointed to the sky. "It's not all darkness out there."

"Stars?"

"Some say our fate is tied to the stars."

He turned from the fire and his head took a quick spin, dehydration, lack of food, and strong drink loosening the weight of gravity. He stared at the massive cluster of lights in the Milky Way, a highway of shimmering sparks smeared across the black sky. He'd never seen the galaxy like this before, so close, so clear, parallel tracks of stars merging and separating, all of it wheeling as one unit across the horizon. It was a secret, he thought, hidden entirely from view when the sun was up, readily forgotten by day. But it was ever present, dominating reality, determining fate, perhaps, its true nature revealed only when the sun went down, only in the alchemy of night. He looked beyond the nebula, into the emptiness that cradled those blazing suns and galaxies all the way to the beginning of time, but as intently as he stared, he still could not fathom it. Never had he felt like such a single, tiny passenger on such a fragile, spinning, speck of a planet as he did right here, in the middle of a desert miles and miles from anyone else. Except for Relic. A stranger who wandered these gorges like some sort of sasquatch, brewed a sharp brand of moonshine, and saved his life.

Brayden cleared his throat. "Do you ever look up there and wonder?" He glanced at Relic. "Is there intelligent life somewhere in the stars?"

"Sure as shit there's intelligent life out there."

Does Relic believe in… UFOs? "How do you know for sure?"

"Cause they're smart enough to steer clear of us assholes."

Brayden suddenly laughed out loud, forgetting Henry, Dylan, everything, wondering instead about little green men with tiny legs and giant brains, watching from afar.

The fire blinked out abruptly, a light switch turned off, leaving only blood-red coals to throb with the heat. Relic added fresh sticks and they caught again, lighting the camp once more with flickers of gold.

"Say," Relic ran a pair of fingers through his goatee. "I have a question for you."

"Yeah? Do I have to answer it?"

"No."

Brayden shrugged.

"You said you're an English major, right?"

Relic asked.

He nodded.

"So, English major, there's something I've been wondering..."

Brayden looked up at Relic.

"Why do 'slim chance,'" he held his hands close together, "and 'fat chance,'" he spread his hands far apart, "appear to mean the same thing?"

Brayden chortled, snorting through his nose.

"You're the expert."

"Sorry."

"Yeah, beats me too." Relic looked into the night, stroking his goatee.

"That's the kind of stuff you wonder about out here?"

"You can't ponder the meaning of life all the time." The flame glistened in his teeth when he smiled.

"No, I guess not." Brayden's shoulders relaxed and he reached for more water. "What brought you here, to this specific canyon? Were you looking for those diamonds?"

"Nope. Didn't know anything about 'em till I heard you and your uncle find them with that Dylan guy."

"So how does the ladder man connect with the diamonds?"

"Just what I was hoping you might know."

Brayden poured more water down his throat and took a breath. "What are a bunch of loose diamonds doing up here anyway? Where did they come from?"

"I don't know just what caused them to be here. But I do have a theory about where they may have come from. And tomorrow, we'll take a look and see."

CHAPTER 34

Barc felt the vibration on his cell phone, waking him at 1:30 a.m. He rubbed the sleep from his eyes and rolled over. He'd camped in just his sleeping bag because the weather looked good and he wanted to be close to the rafting group and out of sight. A tent would have attracted the curious. He'd watched the group from a distance off and on, learning little except that the one he'd identified as Henry was a real talker, going from person to person then back again, working the group like a Washington lobbyist.

Last night, when the sun had set and shadows spread across the canyon, Henry had come and reported that one of the guides planned to float out of the canyon at daylight to bring back law enforcement. It was hard to say how much time would pass before police or the FBI could arrive. Even without the usual stops made with guests, it would take a guide at least one very full day to get from here to the take-out spot, where the dirt road met the river. If no one was there when he arrived, the guide would have to wait until the next day to hope for a ride or access to someone else's sat phone. Then, it might take most of that day for help to helicopter in. That would give Jeb and Ivan only one more day. Although they should be out of Devil's Tail by then, they would still be somewhere on the river when the police arrived. And, it was possible the guide would encounter another group of rafters with a sat phone and call for help even sooner.

No, it seemed he had no choice but to prevent a guide, or anyone else, from rafting down river. There were lots of ways, but Henry had had an idea.

Barc pulled on his wool socks, which held warmth even when wet, and tied the laces on his running shoes. He put his hunting knife on his belt, stretched a black ski cap over his head, and went quietly down to the rafters' camp.

A quarter moon glimmered above the canyon. The river rippled in a slow boil, muscling past the sandstone walls with the unstoppable force of thousands of cubic feet of water per second, its throaty burble drowning out the sounds of his footsteps. The three rafts were tied to separate anchors on shore. Sometimes, guides slept on their rafts at night, but he couldn't see if anyone was in their boats tonight.

Barc slid quietly into the water above the rafts, resisting the urge to groan at the shock of cold. The rafts were tucked into a slight cove by the beach, out of the main current, so the flow was gentle. The water was about four feet deep, so he was able to walk along the bottom, using his arms to stroke against the drift. He lowered himself so that only his head was above the surface.

The first raft soon loomed above him. He used his arms to absorb the soft impact as he touched the upriver side. He could see the wooden oar above him, strapped to the frame in case it jumped from the rafter's hand in the middle of a tussle with the rapids. He lifted his knife and slowly rubbed it against the cotton rope. The raft rose up and down with each stroke so he slowed his pace, gritting his teeth against the frigid water. In moments, the loop fell into a single strand. Quietly, carefully, he lifted the oar from its mount, balancing it along the middle, and pulled it away from the boat. He laid the oar on the surface of the water. But instead of removing and hiding it somewhere, like Henry wanted, Barc guided it out into the flow. In a flash, the oar was sucked into the main current and swept away. Henry had the right idea about how to strand the rafters here, but Barc was going to make it long-term. No need to hide the oars when you could dispose of them completely.

He waded his way to the other side of the first raft and repeated the process. Then he floated to the next boat and stopped to examine the campers on shore. He could smell some lingering smoke and soot, remnants of a blazing fire. Tents were scattered on a shelf of ground above the beach. No flashlights glared. No one was moving.

Barc pulled his knife again and sliced the safety rope on the upriver side of the second raft. He replaced the blade in its sheath, which was under the icy flow. Then, he lifted the oar with both hands and slid it into the current with a mild slap on the surface. He listened, but all remained quiet as the oar was swept away.

He moved to the other side of the raft, the downstream side, and took the same steps. The river was deeper and the current grew stronger here, threatening to pull him away, so he had to lift the oar one-handed while he clung to the raft. He released his hold, the water shifted him from the boat, and he laid the oar in the river, but it just spun in the flow. He walked quietly into even deeper water and shoved the oar outward. At first, it circled in the backwater, but then the wide end touched the hard-moving current and it finally disappeared into the ripples.

He was now at the third and final raft. He pulled his knife from its sheath, the cold making it harder and harder for him to move his fingers properly, but he raised it into the air and sliced the rope on the upstream oar. This time, he set the knife on the side of the boat; getting it in and out of its underwater sheath was becoming difficult. He lifted the oar with both hands, but the flow was more commanding here, sliding his feet along the river bottom, sucking him under the raft. He did the only thing he could: he quickly pushed the oar under him, to help him stay more buoyant, and held his breath. The river slid him and the oar under the bottom of the boat, bumping gently along, his eyes squeezed shut, and he popped out on the other side. Instinctively, he released the oar and reached for the downstream mount and held on, kicking his legs against the flow, slowly, slowly, getting his feet under the raft. His head and ski cap were now soaked in the frigid water, stinging cold constricting his throat, tightening his lungs. He set his legs in a fighting stance on the riverbed, one in front of the other, resisting the water as best he could, but when he reached for the safety rope to cut it, he realized that his knife was still on the other side of the boat.

He reached up for the rope and fumbled for the

place it was tied together, his fingers too stiff for subtle movement, too numb to untwist much of anything, and just when he finally found the knot, a human form sat straight up in a sleeping bag, a rigid board sprung to life, and the person let loose a quick cry of alarm, sending Barc's fingers off the mount, lifting his feet from the river bottom a second time, and spinning him into the empty night.

****

He rolled cold, wet pants down to his ankles, tangling them into his underwear, shivering as he went. It had taken Barc three-quarters of an hour to get to shore and travel past the rafters' campground in a wide arc, moving carefully through the night. He'd reached his rough camp behind a boulder and, though he could not build a fire here, he had some of those chemical heating packets and tossed them into his sleeping bag. Damn it was cold; he could not steady his hands. He slid into the bag naked, and still a little wet, and tore open one heating pack, then another, and held on, waiting for the chill to recede. After a while, his skin began to warm, and then his body core, and he finally began to relax. He'd done what was needed – those rafters weren't going anywhere now.

CHAPTER 35

The sun had begun to touch the north-eastern wall of the canyon, a sliver of gold on the rim far above their camp. An ambient glow lit the meadow, tents, and gurgling river, but the air was still chilled from a cloudless night. Em stood and pulled the hood of her fleece jacket over her head. She cupped her hands to her mouth and blew into them, steamed air warming her fingers for a brief moment.

She walked toward the sound of the water, its glossy sheen a curtain of ink, rippling like a reptile. Voices rounded the curve by their camp kitchen, scraps of sentences, low and worried. She walked toward the river guides, huddled by one of the rafts, and they all stopped talking and watched her.

"Good morning." She nodded.

They all nodded in return.

"Something up?"

Connor looked at Audrey and George then gave them a quick nod.

"Truth is, we could use your help." Audrey adjusted her dark ski cap.

"Yes?"

"But we need to keep it between us, for now."

"Sure, but…"

"Can you agree to that?"

"Of course."

Audrey glanced at Connor. "Well, someone stole our oars in the middle of the night."

"What?"

Connor lifted his finger to his lips.

"Sorry."

"I slept on my raft last night," George pointed to the most downstream raft, "when I felt something underneath it. Woke me from a dead sleep, and I panicked a little bit, sat up, and someone was trying to untie the safety rope that holds the oars to the boat, in case they slip out of our hands in the rapids. Whoever it was sort of jumped backwards and spun away," he circled his hand in the air, "and disappeared."

"Whoa."

"When I started to wake up more, I got my flashlight and looked around. The rope on the other oar had been cut and the oar was gone. A hunting knife was balanced on the boat frame. I don't know why he would have left it there, except by mistake, but it looks like he cut all of the ropes except the one on my right side, next to where I was sleeping. And he took all the oars but that one."

"Holy crap! Why would someone do that?"

"Only one reason I can think of…" Connor crammed his hands into his pockets. "To keep us from going anywhere."

Audrey stomped her feet on the sand. "Why would anyone want to keep us here? I don't get that at all."

"I know one person who wants to keep us here: Henry." Connor shook his head in disgust. "He's been convincing everyone to stay and look for his nephew, but most are staying to collect more diamonds."

"It was dark, I was still half-asleep, but the guy who took the oars did not look like Henry to me. Besides, he was in the water. The fire had died out long ago. He'd have no way to get dry and warm again without one of us noticing, would he?" George scratched the side of his nose.

"Why would Henry care?" Audrey asked. "We agreed that Connor and some others would stay and keep searching for Brayden, and watch over Dylan's body. If Henry wanted that, well, he already had it. Taking the oars wouldn't make any difference."

Em straightened. "Guys." She looked at each of them. "I came to find you this morning to tell you I saw someone watching our camp last night with binoculars."

The guides looked at each other.

"Over by a boulder, up there." She pointed far behind her. "It didn't seem like anyone from our group, but I couldn't see them very well. And I noticed Henry go walking in that guy's direction, though it was getting dark by then. He may have just gone for a walk or to use the porta-potty, but still, it seemed like he was headed toward the man on the boulder."

They stood quietly.

"If you think about it, Audrey's right about Henry." Connor's breath hung before them for a moment, steam expiring in the morning air. "We committed to him that we'd keep looking for Brayden. He already has that promise from us."

"So whoever took the oars wants to keep us from going for *help*." Em's words seemed to jar them all.

"Shit." Connor spun a full circle. "The missing sat phone; it's not missing because it came loose. Someone took it."

"And it could have been anyone in the group." Audrey pointed at Em and shook her head. "Except you."

"Thank you." Em nodded. "But..."

"I'm a pretty good judge of character. And," Audrey raised her finger, "I know your boss and he speaks well of you."

"Really?" Em smiled at the thought.

"Sure." Audrey crossed her arms.

"The guy you saw last night, Em. Could it have been Brayden?" George asked.

"What?"

Audrey drew a quick breath. "Oh, god."

"He could be working with his uncle to keep us here, until after they gather up all the gems." George's hands spread as if holding an open book.

Em shook her head. "The man didn't look like Brayden. Besides, wouldn't they want to leave the canyon whenever they were ready? To do that, they'd have to steal the oars and then hide them, too. The man George saw float away wasn't holding onto a bunch of oars."

"Unless he handed them to Brayden, waiting on the shore."

Em crinkled her nose, a loathsome odor in the wind.

"Or it could be someone outside the group, spying on us all." Connor said.

"Or someone outside in cahoots with someone inside," Audrey added.

"God, this is crazy," George waved his arms. "What in the hell is this all about?"

They all looked at each other and Connor said what they were thinking: "The damned diamonds."

They stood in silence for several moments, considering their situation.

"We really can't send anyone for help?" Em asked.

"Well, we have an emergency oar on Connor's boat." George cleared his throat.

"So, we have one emergency oar plus the regular oar the thief didn't manage to steal, on George's boat?"

"Yep," Audrey nodded. "So, we still have enough oars for one boat. If we leave the equipment behind, all but some tents and snacks, we might cram all the guests onto one raft and get them out of here."

"Should we do that? We should do that!" Em said.

"No." Connor crossed his arms. "Not yet. It's still risky. We'd have no safety boat, no back up if someone got tossed in the rapids. We should try one more time to find Brayden, assuming he's still actually missing. That means me, Henry, and at least a couple more on a search today. Whoever is watching us doesn't seem to know about the emergency oar. Let him think he's got us completely stranded. If we find Brayden today, then all of us need to get out of here – pronto. But before then, we shouldn't tip our hat…"

"And if we don't find Brayden today?" Audrey removed her ski cap and tucked it into her jacket pocket.

Connor raised his brow as if to say, "we'll cross that bridge when we come to it."

"Not a word of this to anyone." Audrey stepped back from the group. "And for now," she pointed at Connor and George, "we have coffee and our famous maple bacon to fry."

"If someone else doesn't fry us first," Connor whispered to the others.

CHAPTER 36

Ivan and Jeb had risen with the sun and worked their way farther up the canyon, above the waterfall and along the little stream. They'd climbed a low ridge and reached the base of the main canyon, spread out before them like a massive picture book, slopes of grass and rock like rumpled pages leading to imposing cliffs in the distance. To their left, a dry creek twisted north and out of sight, so they'd continued to follow the trickling water, the same general direction Ivan had taken to chase the pony-tailed man the day before. They walked slowly, kneeling every few feet to run their fingers through the damp gravel. They continued up the gentle rise until the sun was nearly overhead.

"Any luck?" Ivan stared intently at chips of quartz spread across the palm of his hand.

"None at all." Jeb tossed loose sand to the ground

and stood.

Ivan looked back toward where they'd started. "We've gone maybe two and a half miles by now."

"The last gem I found was a little ruby, back down where this creek and that dry drainage meet." Jeb nodded back down the canyon.

"I'm thinking this creek is not going to lead us to the source."

"I'm thinking you're right."

"We need to hike back down to where that side canyon meets this one. Then follow the dry creek up the side canyon." Ivan pointed.

Jeb nodded. "Yeah."

"No telling how deep that drainage goes, or how hard it will be to hike it."

"No sign of those guys you chased."

"Maybe they know something we don't." Ivan raised his brow.

"Maybe they're already up there, finding the mother lode."

"Then we'd best get a move on." Ivan stood and turned.

"And keep a close eye out for them along the way…"

CHAPTER 37

Sunlight seemed to pry Brayden's eyelids open, and he lay there for a while, staring at the ashes from last night's fire. He sensed Relic moving behind him, so he sat up. The northern branch of Devil's Tail spread before him, a short plain dotted with rusty boulders and jade-colored brush. High cliffs rimmed the canyon, serrated edges close and sharp against the liquid sky. They'd camped several miles up this dry drainage, a crooked path running perpendicular to the little creek that flowed through the larger canyon to the south and west.

He had a thin blanket tangled around his waist and shoulders and it took him a minute to get loose of it.

"You slept well." Relic sat cross-legged by the fire rocks.

"Yeah."

"Took my blanket and snored half the night." Relic

looked at him from under his brow and grinned.

"Oh, sorry." He folded the blanket and handed it to Relic.

"No worries." Relic rolled the cloth tightly and tied it to the bottom of his pack. "Fire kept me warm enough."

"Good."

"Hungry?"

"Starved."

Relic handed Brayden two strips of beef jerky and pointed to his water bottle. "This is breakfast. When you're done, be sure to finish the water. We'll hike up about a half mile from here and resupply at a little spring."

Brayden tore into the first strip.

"Feeling any better today?"

Brayden swallowed. "Like a new man."

Relic nodded and chewed slowly on some jerky of his own.

Brayden reached for his boots, which he'd left by the fire.

"Wait. Shake those out."

"What?"

"Scorpions sometimes get in your boots at night."

"Oh!" Brayden shook his right boot over the ground and a small, translucent scorpion plopped into the dirt. "Holy shit!" The creature circled once then scurried away from camp and out of sight.

"Those things can kill you!" Brayden shook his boot some more then looked carefully into it before he slid it onto his foot.

"Not the ones around here. But they hurt like the devil, and if they sting your hand or your foot, you won't be using it much for a few days." Relic lifted a rock near the fire ring. "See?" he pointed. Two more scorpions, the size of postage stamps, hid beneath the stone.

"They could have crawled all over and stung us last night." Brayden stared at the tiny arachnids.

"Not usually. They don't have much interest in us unless we disturb 'em." Relic reached forward quickly and grabbed one of the scorpions by its tail and held it up. "Harmless if you handle 'em right."

"Shit, man, put that down."

Relic dropped it and placed the rock gently back in place, but he seemed to be thinking about the little creatures.

Brayden shook his left boot upside down, checked it twice, then put it on. He poured the last of his water down his throat.

Relic stood and dusted himself off. He'd re-tied his hair into a tight ponytail and looked fully recharged and refreshed. Sleeping in the dirt actually seemed to agree with the man.

Brayden stood and stretched the kinks from his joints. He walked a yard or so away, turned by a low bush, and urinated.

Much better, he thought.

An early sun lit the western cliffs, hiding the cracks and crags he'd seen last night, blending it all with a watercolor brush full of egg yolk and bronze, paints stirred by the light but not fully blended.

Brayden looked back toward their little camp and Devil's Tail. The canyon narrowed quickly and turned to his right, disappearing behind the curve. The drainage rose steeply at the turn, and he wondered what they would find beyond.

He rejoined Relic, and they began a trek up the faint path, climbing through sandstone blocks, split and rolled into their path by time and erosion.

Before long, despite the cool morning air, Brayden began to sweat. They finished a steep section and arrived at a more level spot. Relic took them into a tumble of large boulders, their edges rounded by the wind and rain, and they suddenly came upon a small pool, only four feet wide. Lush, green ferns suckled on the moisture, anchored loosely on thin layers of soil atop the rock. Long-legged bugs of some sort skated across the surface, busy gathering something even smaller. Moss floated in parts of the stale pool along with all sorts of twigs and algae and unknown biological specimens. Relic put his pack on the ground and sat by the water. Brayden did the same. Relic closed his eyes and seemed to mumble a short prayer.

"We'll take turns sucking the water through my filter."

"That water?" Brayden pointed.

"That water." Relic pulled a water bottle from his bag with a tube-shaped filter down the middle. "May take a while." He pulled the raw water through the tube and into his mouth, then spit it into a nearly empty rubber bladder he'd been drinking from last night. When he'd finally filled it to the brim, he used the same technique to fill his regular water bottle, then the one that had the filter in it.

"Here. Your turn." He wiped the tube with his shirt and handed it to Brayden.

Any other day, any other circumstance, Brayden might have actually declined. But after suffering the day before, he took the filter with a deep appreciation, dipped it into the brackish water and filled his bottle the way Relic had shown him. When they were done, they each took a deep drink that tasted of stale gym socks.

After a basketball game.

Yes, Brayden thought, his relationship with water was certainly evolving.

"This little spring used to be deeper and flow out of here 'till late summer. See the ring around here," he pointed to a gray line that ran along the sandstone, a foot above the water level. "The water used to be up to there, with a flow to it that kept it cleaner." He stared into the stagnant pool.

"What happened to it?"

"Seven billion people burning eleven billion metric tons of oil every year. 'Climate change,' folks call it now, that's what happened to it. Glaciers evaporating, temperatures rising," he pointed his hand upward, "springs drying up, lakes shrinking, the mighty Colorado River twenty percent lower than usual, this year."

"I didn't realize. I mean, not the specifics..."

"Well, there's just too damn many of us humans. Growth for the sake of growth is the ideology of a cancer cell. That's from Edward Abbey, another smart man." He raised a finger. "The elders say that to honor the Creator you have to honor his creations. All the earth is our home, our nest, and we are all of one spirit in its many forms. But most humans have that ideology of a cancer cell. The philosophy of a coronavirus. The earth can't keep supporting us all unless we change our ways, take hard action. Should've been done long ago," he grumbled. "And life here in this desert is going to shrink; the tadpoles and frogs and bugs are going to die out, and they're just the first of us to go."

Brayden scanned the circle around the little spring, grass clinging to the sides, insects skimming the edges, rugged moon-rocks dominating the land beyond the perimeter.

"Don't get me started on how fast we humans can screw things up."

Brayden wondered if Relic would have to leave these canyons. Without springs like this dotting the landscape, even a hardened hermit could not survive in the desert. "This is all happening now, isn't it? In real time?"

"Real time?"

"Yeah."

"You mean, the time in this dimension?" Relic tilted his head.

"Yeah..." Brayden stretched the word until it became half a question.

"Is it possible for time to be anything *other* than real?"

"No, no," Brayden shook his head, "I mean it's happening right now, even as we sit here."

"Oh." Relic straightened his back. "Yes, of course. Everything that's happening is happening now."

"Right. Sorry." Brayden grimaced. How long has this guy been wandering around out here?

"Wait." Relic smiled, signaling a change of subject. He pulled a bag from his pack, opened it, and poured hard, oval candies into Brayden's palms.

"M&M's?"

"Peanut. Only the best trail food known to man." Relic popped some into his mouth, his cheeks round and full, his grin like a cherub enjoying a perfect meal, and it made Brayden smile.

He slid the candies into his mouth, crunched deeply into the salty chocolate, and mushed them over his tongue. Relic was right, and that thought made him smile, too.

"Up beyond this bend," Relic pointed. He stood and re-shouldered his pack. Brayden did the same and they resumed their hike up the canyon. Brayden strained to keep up, already hot and sweaty again, the M&M's making him thirsty. His feet felt like they'd been tenderized, his thighs sore and stiff. They pushed higher and higher as the cliffs closed more tightly around them and, after a while, Relic stopped and stared. Brayden climbed to the spot next to him and gazed across the opening.

Flattened against the ground, hidden in a rocky gorge maybe sixty feet across, was some kind of pattern. More than that, a T-shaped remnant of something man-made, a block of rusted metal at the front of it, shapes and boxes and rags strewn behind it. Then he saw something else.

There, just below the metal block, were the sun-bleached bones and balding skulls of what were once two human beings.

CHAPTER 38

"What's this?" Brayden stepped toward the skeletons.

"Crash site. I've seen this before, from a distance. It's the only man-made thing around from this century, the only source of those diamonds that I can figure." Relic combed his fingers through his goatee. "We'll need to take a closer look."

"Oh, man," Brayden whispered to himself. The ground levelled out here, curving into an arrow-shaped flat before it abruptly ended at a point higher up. A "box" canyon with no way out. Brayden followed Relic as he wound his way to the site.

The engine block became obvious as they approached, narrow fins of its air-cooled cylinders corroding in the sand. The tip of a split propeller pointed to the sky, still clinging to its aspirations. Forward edges of the wings touched the wooden ribs that gave it shape, but only scant bits of cloth clung here and there, along the fastened joints.

They stopped and stared at the wreckage. The bodies were unnerving at first, but as he watched them, they became macabre curiosities, sights he couldn't pull away from. Two skulls lay partially buried in sand, each with a little skin and hair still attached. Bones fanned out behind them, disconnected puzzles scattered by wind and rain. Two small bundles of cloth had slid farther down the gentle incline, canvas backpacks rotted away, their contents spread along a tangle of sun-bleached wooden spars that must have been the tail of the airplane. A metal box of some sort winked in the morning sun.

Relic stepped closer to the debris and began examining it.

"What could have caused them to crash?" Brayden scanned the site.

"Could be anything, really. Ran out of gas. Flew into a storm. Engine trouble."

"Right."

"We'll never know for sure." Relic picked his way toward the propeller.

Brayden went to the metal box and knelt next to it. He dug the sand around it and lifted it out. The thing was made of tin, a black background with faded green lettering, the label "Belfast Cut Plug" still clear, the word "cigar" half flaked away. The lid was closed and hinged on one side. He pried and twisted and pulled until it began to slide and finally opened.

He peered inside and his chest clenched.

"What did you find?" Relic stepped closer.

"You were right!" Brayden held the tin into the light. Emeralds, rubies, and diamonds shined in the bright sun, packed tightly into the felt-lined tin.

"Shit on a shingle!"

"There must be millions in here!"

"Or a shit load!"

"There must be more. There must be another one of these tins that broke up, that let the diamonds wash down the canyon."

"Right."

Brayden carefully closed the old cigar tin and set it aside.

"Here!" Relic pointed to another tin twelve feet away, about the same size, its artwork scoured to raw metal. The box was open and empty. A small, dry gulley showed where the water ran when it rained, across the open area and then down the steep drainage that led back to the main canyon and, from there, to the little creek and pond where the rafting group had stopped to wade.

Relic followed the old flow lines, picking up pieces of gravel as he went, occasionally pocketing what Brayden figured were more gems.

If the open box was as full as the one on the ground in front of him, the find was worth several million dollars, scattered all down the canyon. What if there were more boxes?

Brayden found a flat rock by his feet and began to dig into the sand and dirt near the two tins they'd found. He soon worked up a sweat, the salty taste of it dripping to his lips. He wanted to drink more water but could not curb his enthusiasm; the excitement of discovering gems in the dusty bottom of this narrow canyon was too intoxicating.

He hit something metal, but it turned out to be a belt buckle. He searched closer to the tail of the airplane and struck another buckle of a different kind, one used for a seat belt. The thought of it wrapped around the waist of one of the fliers made his stomach flinch, but he kept digging through the sand until he hit another cigar box, rectangular, with the remains of a woman's image on the front, scarf around her head.

"Relic!" He pushed the sand away and lifted the container onto his lap. This lid was not hinged and it popped off quickly. There, stuffed as full as the first, was a thick mosaic of glistening diamonds. What the hell were these two fly-boys doing carrying cigar tins full of gems across the desert? Was it some sort of secret delivery? A jewel heist gone sour?

"Relic!"

"Shush!" Relic trotted to Brayden, finger on his lips.

Brayden held up the third cigar tin.

"We have to go. I can hear two people working their way up the canyon. Not far," Relic whispered.

"Shit."

"Yeah."

Brayden closed the tin tightly and slung his pack to the ground. He placed both full boxes into his pack and zipped it shut.

"Fill in the holes where you dug up the tins." Relic pointed. "Hurry."

Brayden scooped loose soil into the depressions left by the cigar boxes and smoothed them over as best he could. "How the hell are we going to get out of here?"

"Quickly. Back the way we came, there's a ledge we can get to and hope they don't see us. We'll hide as they go by."

"What are our chances?"

He scratched his goatee. "Right now, I'd say they're pretty fat."

CHAPTER 39

"Work your way along there," Relic pointed to a ridge several feet above them. "Go as high as your gut will take you."

Brayden pulled the straps tightly on his pack and ran to the bottom, searching for a way up. The low cliff was cracked and uneven, ledges reaching out from the rock for several feet then disappearing back into the wall. He worked his way up the first, then the next, until he came to a long ledge below the main cliff, which towered above him another three hundred feet. He glanced back for a moment.

Relic seemed to be gathering something from under rocks along the drainage, picking things up and dropping them into a plastic bag of some sort. What was he doing?

Brayden searched ahead and began to walk along

the narrow ledge. The canyon dropped off quickly below him, the height lifting him, it seemed, in a moment of vertigo. He put his right hand on the cliff, focused ahead, and continued toward a patch of level ground well above the trail.

Boots stumbled against rock, men coming up the canyon to find them and the diamonds. Brayden looked back the way he'd come, the canyon walls narrow until they reached the site of the crash, where they widened then came to a sharp point at the end of the box canyon. He suddenly realized how the canyon got its name – the end of it was shaped like a Devil's Tail.

He moved quickly to a grassy spot behind a couch-sized rock and settled in, waiting for the men to come higher into the canyon and pass him. Where the hell was Relic?

Just then, Relic came trotting into view, keeping close to the cliff. He reached Brayden and kneeled behind the same chunk of sandstone.

"Does this canyon ever end?" The question came from a voice below them. Brayden peered around the rock. Ladder man had stopped and wiped his forehead.

"Hey!" The man who had the pistol stood a few feet ahead of ladder man and searched the ground. "Tracks…"

Ladder man looked up as Brayden ducked back

behind the rock.

"Jeb! Up there!"

"They're trying to double back on us, Ivan."

"The hell they will."

Brayden heard boots scramble across the ground beneath them.

"Show yourself or we're coming up there now!"

Shit, no, Brayden thought, they should run for it, right now! He looked at Relic, who turned and removed his pack. He fumbled with something inside and pulled out a small waterproof bag about the size of a large envelope and held it up for Brayden to see. But the bag was yellowish and opaque; Brayden could not see what was in it.

"I'm going to try something," Relic whispered. "Stay put."

Brayden nodded.

"Hey, guys, you got us! I'm going to come out now, so don't shoot!" Relic stood slowly, arms raised in the air.

"You!" Ivan blurted.

"Who?" Jeb turned to Ivan.

"No one," Ivan lowered his voice, "just someone I've seen before, in the back country."

Jeb looked back up the slope. "Who else is with you?"

"One of the rafters."

"He needs to stand up."

Relic motioned for Brayden to stand, so he rose above the waist-high rock, arms above his head.

"Come down from there now!" Ivan shouted.

"No." Relic waved Brayden to shelter behind the rock again. "But we have what you want."

"What do you have?" Jeb aimed his pistol at Relic.

"We found the source of the diamonds. Up there." He pointed. "At the end of the canyon, there's an old plane wreck. We found loose diamonds all over there and gathered them into a dry bag." Relic lowered himself, picked up the bag, and held it over his head.

"Toss that down here!"

"We want to make a deal."

"What deal?" Jeb spread his arms.

"We toss you the bag. You let us get off this ridge and back to camp. No shooting anyone, not us, not anyone in the group."

"Or what?"

"Or we'll keep climbing out of here and you'll never get us. Or the diamonds." Relic lowered the bag to the top of the rock. Brayden rose and peeked over.

"Ivan, get over here!"

Ivan and Jeb huddled and spoke in hurried whispers, shaking and nodding their heads. After a few moments, they both looked up at Relic and Brayden.

"You got a deal if the diamonds are in it. Toss the bag down here. We're still going to find this plane crash you say is up here. Then we'll leave this canyon. You'll be ahead of us and can go your merry way. No one gets shot."

"No…" Brayden whispered, touching the bag Relic was holding. "They'll double-cross us…"

CHAPTER 40

Henry rounded a corner in the trail where it left the open plain. He began its winding path through brush and rock and stopped to join Carl, who leaned against a large boulder. They were both well ahead of the others, on their way back to the little creek where they'd found diamonds the day before.

"Getting hot already, huh?" Henry put his hand on the rock and leaned at the waist.

"Yeah."

"Say, Carl, is everything all right?"

"What? Sure."

"OK. Sorry, I just wondered."

Carl glared at him.

"Well, it seems like Claire is not so happy today, that's all." He straightened. "None of my business, really, just noticed it is all."

"Everything's good. Why wouldn't it be? We're about to be rich enough to travel the world." His teeth flashed in a grin.

"Right, well, save some for me, will you?"

"What?"

"I have to look for my nephew, you know."

"Well, I could grab a couple of diamonds for you, I guess."

"Good man."

"But to be honest, you ought to get your own, Henry."

"Have to take it to make it, right?"

"Something like that."

"I get it, I do." Henry checked behind him. "But listen, the need to look for Brayden is what got Connor and the other guides to agree to this little expedition today."

Carl narrowed his eyes. "You don't think you're going to find Brayden, do you?"

Henry took a breath. "No. Not really."

"I think he ran off to find the source." Carl scanned the trail. "I think I ought to follow that stream up into the canyon, too, and see what's up there. He didn't come back because he found the mother lode."

"Connor would have a fit."

"Yeah, I don't give a shit about Connor, but I do need him to keep us fed and sheltered and get us out of here, when the time comes. I figure we don't have that much leverage. Gotta get all we can while we can – which is today."

Henry shifted his weight. "That's about how I see it, too. I plan to go up the canyon with Connor to look for Brayden, but I'll also be checking along the creek. If the diamonds just keep showing up, I'll gather what I can and let you know. Maybe it's worth trying to come back again tomorrow."

"In that case, you need to grab a couple diamonds for me." Carl raised his brow.

"What happened to 'every man for himself'?"

"Right. But still, if you hear me trying to get people up here for another day, you'll know I found more upstream. You should support me on that."

"Fair enough."

"You're not going to let your nephew slow you down, are you?"

Henry thought for a moment. "Not any more than your little filly is going to slow you down."

Carl's lip curled in a crooked grin. "You have to take it to make it, huh?"

Henry nodded and started back up the trail.

CHAPTER 41

Relic narrowed his dark eyes at Brayden and gave him a quick nod, a gesture of assurance. Brayden knew just then how much he'd come to trust the man, this sasquatch of the desert. He lifted his hand off the bag.

"OK. Here it comes." Relic stepped away from the rock and swung his arm back, forward, and back again, leveraging the toss. He released as it rose on its arc and it spun through the air and landed on the trail near Ivan's feet.

Jeb put his pistol into a shoulder holster and watched as Ivan unrolled the top of the plastic container.

Relic turned and re-shouldered his pack.

Ivan reached in and pulled a handful of something out and began searching through it. Jeb's grin turned into a victory laugh as he gazed into the bag. Then Ivan flung his hand away, pain racking his face.

"Shit, oh my god, oh my god." Ivan's left hand squeezed his right, shaking it violently and he stumbled away from the trail, screaming and swearing like a mad man.

"What the hell?" Jeb stepped toward Ivan.

"Time to go." Relic pointed farther along the ridge and pushed Brayden forward. "I gave 'em a bag of pebbles, with a few diamonds on top…and two little scorpions in with it all."

Brayden turned and stared at him, mouth open.

"Just wanted to fatten up our chances some."

Brayden spun forward again, peering between the boulders, watching the men below. Ivan lay curled on the ground, whimpering. Jeb's lips twisted grotesquely in a mask of primitive anger. He turned and reached for something in Ivan's pack, pulled it out, yanked something from it, and stepped back to throw.

The dark, round object soared toward them in a high, slow arc that made Brayden stare as it floated upward then down, down toward them until Relic shoved him forward along the ledge, away from the incoming object, away from the rock they'd hidden behind.

Ba-boom!

The explosion expelled all other sounds from the narrow canyon, concussing his skull, blasting and deafening him at the same time, rocking his chest, throwing him forward. The ground suddenly turned to liquid, his feet churning through a gumbo of sand, gravel, and sage, sliding together down the slope at breakneck speed, the mass of it skidding toward the tiny trail they'd come up. He tried to keep his head above the surging mass, swimming desperately through it all as it came to rest thirty feet below, all in one frantic instant, and now he lay buried to his neck in dirt and sand, a chunk of sandstone the size of a suitcase pushed against his head. Dust hung in the air, quiet, unmoving, suffocating.

Shock kept Brayden from moving or breathing for several moments, until the reflexive need to breathe forced the air from his lungs and he gasped. His arms and legs were buried, and he lay on his back, his body horizontal. He tried to move his head but the rock seemed to slide farther along, pulled more tightly against his ear by gravity, bending his neck to the side. He could see the stone, but he couldn't see up the trail, where Jeb and Ivan would be. A shiver of panic jarred through his muscles, a misfire of neurons, but he took another breath and tried to be still, to figure out what to do next.

Brayden listened for any voices.

"You'll be OK." It sounded like Jeb, several yards away.

"Like hell, I will!"

"It'll hurt for a day or two but you'll live."

"Easy for you to say."

"Here, these are painkillers. Take them."

The voices were quiet for a moment.

"OK, let's get to the end of this canyon."

"Shit, I can't use my hand."

"Hold onto it with your good hand. The pills will start working soon."

"What the hell did you do?"

"Used the grenade I gave you."

"What? Really?"

"Those assholes are dead and buried. The bag of diamonds only has a few on top – the rest of it is just gravel."

"Shit."

"Let's get up to that site and see if they were lying about the plane crash. We can check their bodies for diamonds on the way back down."

Brayden held his breath. He could hear boots on the trail, stomping farther away as they moved up Devil's Tail. Soon, they would be around the corner and out of sight.

"Slow down…"

"Hurry up…"

Their voices faded away.

The stone that had wedged tightly against his head slid farther down the slope, pinning his ear to his right shoulder, shoving his neck into an ever more excessive angle and he thought it would crack his upper spine if it moved any farther. Breathing became more difficult, his airway crimped by the extreme slant.

Slowly, he began to move his right arm upward through the soil, shaking off the sand bit by bit. When his hand was clear, he dug the dirt away from his neck and shoulders and twisted away from the rock, which then slid over the spot where his head had been a moment earlier.

"Jeeez," he whispered. He rose to a seated position and pulled his legs from the loose earth, one at a time, then brushed himself off as best he could. The skin on his ankles had been scoured by the dry sand, lightly bleeding in places, his hands desiccated, his pants a whole new shade of ground-in, reddened dust.

Peering past the rock, he examined the canyon. The trail was partially buried for several yards where the earth had slid from the top. The large rock they'd hid behind earlier, where Relic had thrown the bag of diamonds and scorpions, had rolled halfway downhill and now rested against some smaller rocks just above the trail.

Where the hell was Relic?

Brayden stood carefully, stretching his arms and legs, shaking more dust from his clothes. His pack was still on his back, so he slid it off, brushed it clear of loose dirt, and re-shouldered it. The slide had come to rest at a uniform slant, but tufts of grass and brush, torn from their roots, rose at odd angles from the dirt. Rocks had also rolled from the cliff above, now islands of debris perched precariously on the virgin slope.

Relic had pushed him just before the blast, away from the rock they'd hidden behind; he must be near that same rock. Brayden stood carefully and walked to the sandstone chunk that now rested halfway toward the trail, searching the ground for signs of life. He moved up the path, above the rock, then circled back toward it. There, above the stone, was part of a human form, a head, one arm, one leg, all covered in dust and sand. He ran toward Relic and knelt next to him.

"Hey, hey." He grabbed his arm and shook it. "Relic! Wake up!" He dug loose soil from around his neck and blew the dust away from his face but his eyelids remained flaccid, lifeless.

"Wake up, wake up." He put a finger below Relic's nostrils, waiting, praying for the warmth of his breath.

But he couldn't feel anything at all.

CHAPTER 42

"Ha!" Carl knelt and examined a ruby the size of his fingernail, slipped it into his pants pocket, and giggled, Em thought, like a four-year-old.

"Hon," Claire tried to interrupt his reverie. "I'm going to go with Em up the canyon a ways, to keep looking for Brayden."

Carl waited a beat then waved absently in her direction. Madison wandered along the opposite side of the little creek, her eyes to the ground. Two of the passengers in her raft, Brent and Wes, knelt near the water, their attention divided between a frantic search for gems and a hopeful glance at Madison's yellow hotpants.

Em nodded for Claire to follow her and walked away from the group. They'd debated last night what to do today until Connor, Audrey, and George learned that the oars had been taken during the night. Someone was watching and wanted them to stay in this canyon, without help from anyone else. And with Brayden still missing, and Henry stirring up a hearty lust for diamonds, they seem preordained to spend the day searching for both. Em had gone a long ways down a narrow path that paralleled the main trail, back towards the river, climbing ridges and circling around boulders, but found no sign of Brayden. She'd eventually given up and made her way back to the brook, where most of the group still hovered about, sifting through the sand. But Em had had enough of the fortune hunters, and maybe Claire had, too.

She and Claire hiked upstream toward a jumble of large boulders, cleaved from the cliffs above and slid downhill by gravity and a century of heavy spring rains. They hastened a bit past the stacked stones marking Dylan's grave, keeping it in their periphery. They moved from one rock to the next, peering behind each one, searching around and around them until they met in an open area secluded from the group.

"Nothing," Em declared.

"Footprints all over." Claire pointed.

"Yeah, I think Henry and Connor have been over this ground already."

"Should we keep going?"

"I'd rather look for Brayden than grovel by the

creek." Em glanced from under her brow.

Claire smiled and nodded.

"Let's try up this way." Em swung her arm as if to open a door. "Higher up."

"I still don't understand how Brayden could go missing. I mean, how could he have gone so far from the group?"

"I don't understand it either. Unless he was looking for the source of the diamonds."

"But wouldn't he have turned back by nightfall?"

"If he could have, yeah. That's what has me concerned." Em hurried through the boulders to a place where the view opened wide and the stream nearly disappeared, its braided waters spread across the rocky ground. They trudged upward toward a saddle, of sorts, pushing to get above it. At the top, they rested to catch their breath.

To the west, higher along the little creek, the canyon faded into a sepia haze, the sun past its zenith, glaring at them, and the distance seemed beyond what a person could hike in a whole day. To the north, a ridge of sandstone rose like the spine of a dinosaur and curved out of sight.

A noise, a shuffle of feet, reached them and they turned to look. Connor cupped his hands to his mouth and shouted, "Brayden!" Henry yelled for his nephew in another direction but no one answered. They shuffled toward the creek, eyes on the ground, tired, defeated. In moments, they reached Claire and Em and stopped to rest.

"Nothing?" Em tucked her hair behind her ear.

Connor shook his head. "This canyon is huge."

"How far did you go?" Claire pointed behind him.

"As far as we thought our legs could take us," Henry said, shifting his weight. "Way up there, and along there, to the south, then back." He waved toward the main canyon then let his arm flop to his side. "Everywhere."

"What about north?" Em asked.

"We went a ways up and yelled, but that drainage is dry except during spring run-off." Connor brushed the dust from his shirt. "No water. I can't imagine why Brayden would go that direction, and on the map it looks like a box canyon."

"He can't have just disappeared."

"That's exactly what he's done," Henry swung his head back and forth, staring at the ground.

"Well, we can't stay here any longer." Connor waved toward the western cliffs. "The sun will be down by the time we get everyone all the way back to camp."

They stood there for a moment. Em felt the weight

of defeat, a sense that Brayden had gone too far astray and fallen or twisted an ankle, dead or dying somewhere. And though she felt sorrow for that, she felt some anger, too. What the hell did he think he was doing? Chasing diamonds? They already had one man dead – Dylan – and now almost certainly another.

And what about the man watching their camp? Was there another possibility? Had Brayden been captured by people spying on them? Were they hiding from them? For what purpose? It had to be connected to those damn diamonds, but she could not imagine just what their plan might be.

Connor waved them forward, and they followed him back along the creek, over the saddle, and back toward the jumble of boulders. As they worked their way along, a muffled *thump* sounded in the distance, so faint Em wasn't sure she'd really heard it. She stopped to listen.

Connor turned toward her. "Rockslide, way off. I've heard them before, when a rock balanced on the side of a cliff finally falls off."

Em nodded and they resumed their trek back to the others.

CHAPTER 43

Deputy Dawson rowed casually to the right shore and felt his raft slide across the sandy bottom to a stop. He set the oars on his raft and wiped the sweat from his forehead. Across the river was a wide, unnamed canyon then a long stretch of cliffs that came right down to the water. He pulled his map from his pack and spread it across his knees. If he remembered correctly, another canyon with some nice ruins lay on the left side of the river, several miles down. He could camp there for the night or move on to Hangman Canyon, a hot, desolate spot but with plenty of level ground to pitch a tent.

For the next ten or twelve miles, the right side of the river offered boulder fields and high, ragged cliffs. Not a lot for rafting groups to stop and examine. River left, however, had the next two canyons, unnamed on the maps, then Hangman, then Devil's Tail, each with places to camp and explore.

He hadn't come across a single group so far, the stillness of the empty canyons quieting his thoughts, slowing the hurried pace of life. But he would come to someone eventually, and he resolved to stop and talk with whoever he found.

He took a long drink of warm water and set the bottle back on the floor of his raft. He raised the oars again and began to push away from shore. Hangman Canyon would be a good place to stop tonight if he didn't find anyone between here and there. He leaned his back into the stroke and rowed toward the other side of the river.

CHAPTER 44

Brayden stared down the canyon, past the landslide caused by the grenade, into the haze that veiled the distant southern flats. He couldn't believe it. Those diamond-lusting thieves had killed the hermit of these remote canyons, a man living off the land and his own ingenuity, harming no one, protecting petroglyphs and historic sites from the likes of Ivan and Jeb, protecting tourists like him, saving him even from his own ignorance. His eyes welled with tears and he thought, hell, he'd just cry and cry and cry, all by himself, until he dehydrated into a pile of dust, his mummified remains staring all night at the Milky Way, alone with the fliers in their derelict cloth and wooden airplane, all of them lost in the Devil's Tail.

A wave of sadness shook him, sucking him toward despair. He hung his head onto his chest and thought he could stop breathing right then and there and not even notice. No one would notice.

The moments seemed to stretch into eternity.

Cawf!

Brayden's head jerked upward.

"What's a guy gotta do to get a hand around here?"

Brayden turned and sucked a deep breath of air. "Relic?"

"In real time, so to speak." Relic's head bobbed forward, but the rest of him seemed glued in place.

"Shit!" Brayden wiped his eyes.

"No shit." Relic coughed again. "Give me a hand?"

"Yes, yes, of course." Brayden scrambled toward him and began to dig at the dirt and rocks, moving them away from Relic's left shoulder and arm. Relic began to lift his hand from the dirt as Brayden shifted to his other arm, and soon Relic was helping push and lift and shake the sand from his chest.

"Oh my god, oh my god, I thought you were gone!"

"Not yet." Relic pulled his legs from under the dirt and gravel and began to brush them off.

"Are you OK?"

Relic lifted his arms above his head and brought them back down quickly, grunting. "Think I may have cracked a rib."

"Oh…"

Relic stretched gently upward until his eyes closed and his teeth clenched and he grunted again. He twisted at the waist to his left, then his right, wincing.

"Yep. Bruised or cracked a rib or two." He filled his lungs with air. "Not too bad, though. I can breathe pretty well."

"You've done this before? Broken your ribs?"

"Yep."

Brayden examined Relic for a moment. "Can you walk OK?"

"A little slower than usual."

"Maybe I can keep up with you now."

"Huh." Relic's lips rose in a quick smile. "Seen those assholes anywhere?"

"No."

"If brains were taxed, those guys would get a rebate."

"Huh!" Brayden agreed, amazed at how easily Relic turned these deadly enemies into a corny joke.

"Find us a small branch from a bush, will you?"

Brayden searched about and found a broken sage. He twisted part of it away from the rest and held it up.

"That'll do. Can you push the dirt back here, where I was buried, and fill it in, smooth it out? So it doesn't look like I was here at all."

Brayden nodded and went about the work, kneeling on the ground, scooping sand back into the gaps where Relic had been, leveling the soil. His hands were dry and cracked, dust clogging the blood that rose from splits between his fingers, but he ignored the sting of it. He took the sage and swept it over the top, blending it with the surrounding earth. Then he went back up and repeated the process, hiding his own imprint and footsteps.

"Can you keep doing that as we go down the trail?"

"Sure."

"You know, when I first saw the ladder man – Ivan – he went back to two other men."

"Two?"

"The third man could be in the main canyon, searching for diamonds there. Or, he could be back at their camp, along the river."

"With a gun and a grenade of his own?"

"Waiting in case we come back. Or watching the rafter's camp, the people you are with."

"Damn." Brayden forced the air through his teeth.

"We gotta get moving…"

They hiked steadily along, Brayden sweeping away their footprints as they went.

Two hours later, they reached the shallow creek and walked upstream a few dozen yards, the sun dipping closer to the western rim.

Relic turned into a grassy area strewn with boulders the size of cars, shaved from the cliffs and spread downhill over the centuries. They continued through them as they curved right then ended suddenly at the foot of the weirdest rocks Brayden had ever seen. Before them stood a group of hoodoos, strange spires of sandstone stacked twenty feet tall like scoops of ice cream, vanillas, coffees, and butter pecans, melted onto themselves then freeze-dried in place. Pockets of sand filled depressions along the stone floor of the formation, but otherwise the ground appeared as a single, solid stone, an undulating wave of petrified dunes. Brayden stared at the silent columns for several moments as Relic made his way into them. Brayden followed until they found a shady spot deep among the spires and set their packs on the ground.

"Incredible. Do we stay here for the night?"

"Yep. We're out of sight here. I don't think we could reach your camp before nightfall, anyway. And we might run into that third man, the one with Ivan and Jeb."

"I'd rather not do that tonight. I'm exhausted." Brayden leaned forward, his hands on his knees.

"Can you wrangle some wood for a fire?"

"Yeah." Brayden gathered branches and sticks for a while, dropping them into a pile at the base of one of the spires. Relic unpacked the blanket, a woolen cap, and extra clothes then found rocks for a fire ring and arranged them on the sandstone floor. When they had their makeshift camp as ready as they could, they sat across from each other. Relic broke the branches into smaller pieces and arranged them in the fire pit.

"What's our next move?"

"Put on all our extra clothes and eat something." Relic rooted through his pack. "This is the last of the jerky. We'll have the last of the M&M's for breakfast."

"What I meant was, what are we going to do about the situation?"

"Eat first." Relic handed him two long strips of barbequed beef.

They chewed on the salted meat and on the problems of the diamonds, the rafters, and the thieves.

Relic wiped his hands on his pants. "I'm pretty sure that Jeb and Ivan will still be up at the crash site tonight. Even if they're part way back down, they're not likely to be close to the rafters yet."

Brayden nodded.

"In the last day or so, your group has probably

been watched by the third man. But would the group have gone for help?"

"Yes. I think Connor, the lead guide, said they had a satellite phone."

"So, they could have called for help yesterday afternoon, after you found Dylan's body."

"Which could mean that help has already arrived."

"Or, they could have had some of the group float on down without you, also to get help."

"Same result, then – help could be here already or by tomorrow morning."

"What we don't know is what, if anything, the third man has been doing. Or your uncle, for that matter..."

"Why do you ask about Henry?"

"Well, do you trust him to do the right thing?"

CHAPTER 45

Claire laid her fingers on Carl's arm. "We have enough diamonds right now to afford both: a really nice wedding and to go to Italy on our honeymoon. Don't we?"

"I don't know." He pulled the gems from his pocket and fingered through them.

"Your grandfather was a jeweler. Can you tell what they're worth?"

Carl thought for a moment, staring toward the evening cliffs, then refocused. "We now have," he counted, "seven diamonds and a small ruby. Maybe they are worth seven thousand, retail? I really don't know."

"That's plenty, Carl."

"No. We need a lot more. A nice wedding will cost us over thirty thousand."

She looked to her feet, disappointment in her eyes.

"If we could get back up to the pool tomorrow..."

"Maybe..." She just wanted to find Brayden and leave.

"I'll go check around, see what I can find out about the plan for tomorrow."

"Henry says he wants to go back up to try to find his nephew, Brayden."

"That works," Carl nodded. "I'll go talk to Henry."

"Stay and sit with me a while?" She motioned an invitation.

"I won't be long." Carl stood and moved toward the camp kitchen and other guests, milling about.

The sun slipped gently behind the horizon, lighting the air in an electric, auburn glow, molecules buzzing in the air. Small bats swooped up the evening bugs in a series of glides and dives, their tiny wings beating in a blur.

Carl couldn't see Henry anywhere. Connor was busy stacking driftwood for a fire. Madison seemed at loose ends, momentarily free from any conversation. He went quickly to her.

"Beautiful evening, isn't it?" He motioned for her to sit in a camp chair and pulled another one next to hers.

"Yes."

"Hey, I've been looking closely at the jewels I found today, and came up with an estimate of their value."

"Really?"

"Yeah, my grandfather was a jeweler and I'm not an expert, but based on the number and size, I think I have about seven thousand dollars' worth." He pulled them out of his pocket and let her lean closer to inspect them.

"Can you tell me what mine are worth?"

"Happy to try it." He tucked his gems away.

Madison pulled several stones from one pocket, then more from another one, dumping them into Carl's cupped hand.

"These are a little unorganized. You've got several little pebbles in here, too. See?" He separated some larger, sharp-edged pieces of sand and held his palm toward her.

"Oh! So, I don't have as many as I thought?"

"No, see these," he pushed them away from the others, "some of these aren't gems at all. They're chips of silica or quartz." He had about twelve of them in his hand.

"Oh," her lips rolled into a pout and she looked away.

He quickly covered two diamonds and some sand under his thumb. He reached for her hand and she held it out to him. With his index finger, he pushed four gems from his palm into hers. "But you have, let's see, four really nice sized diamonds here."

Her eyes narrowed and for a flash Carl wondered

if she'd noticed what he'd done, but then she smiled and leaned closer. Despite the fact they'd been camping, he could smell lilac perfume in her hair.

"I'd say you have about four thousand dollars here."

"Whoa." She straightened her back. "Four thousand?"

"As high as, yes."

"Oh, man."

"But there's more to be had up there, at that little creek above the pond, right?"

"Yes, I've been hoping we can get back up there."

"Me, too. Let's each of us talk to Connor about it. See if we can convince him."

"Yes." She tucked the diamonds back into her pocket.

"I'm going to tell him we need to help find Brayden, too, so we may as well kill two birds with one stone. So to speak."

"Yes, I'll do that, too. And Carl?"

"Yeah?"

"What if we pooled our gems together, you and me?"

"Pooled them?" He caught his breath.

"Well, I'm thinking of getting back to civilization after this trip, maybe take a real vacation in Madeira or Sicily. We could save some money if we went together..."

He tensed. "Intriguing idea."

"Just something to think about..."

"Yes," his head bobbed. "Something to think about." He lifted his closed hand. "I'll toss these little rocks. But you keep those four in a safe place."

"Thank you, Carl. I appreciate it." Her eyes seemed to glow in the twilight, energized and earnest. He tried not to notice her legs but couldn't help himself. "Best put some leggings on or you'll freeze tonight." He pointed to her short pants.

"You're right. Thanks again." She stood and turned.

"No problem." He pocketed the two diamonds that had been under his thumb. Did she suspect? That could explain why she wanted to share their resources – she knew he was going to be ahead of the game. Would the slight-of-hand trick work on anyone else? She sauntered toward the beach, hips swaying with the curves along the path.

The last of an ambient sunlight drifted deeply into space. Connor had started a blazing campfire, its flames making objects outside the ring of light seem especially dark.

Henry walked toward Carl and sat in the chair Madison had used. "Good evening."

"Good evening. I was looking for you earlier."

"Oh? How's everything going?" Henry clasped his hands together.

"Pretty well. Found nine gems today, worth eight or nine thousand."

"That's great."

"How about you? My grandfather was a jeweler, and I could give you an estimate of their value."

"I did all right. No thanks on the appraisal, though, I've got a pretty good idea what they're worth."

"OK."

"Besides, I'd rather focus on getting back to that little creek again tomorrow."

"You too?"

Henry nodded. "I've been talking to the others, seeing if they would help me look for Brayden, pointing out to them that they could look for more diamonds while they were up there."

"Like I told you earlier, count me in."

"Good man." Henry leaned toward Carl. "Hey, I've been thinking about something you might want to consider, too."

"Yes?"

"Well, Dylan is dead." He waited a beat. "Brayden is missing and, god willing, will come back to us and he'll be OK."

"Yes, of course."

"So, what will happen when we get back to the take-out spot, off the river, at the end of the trip? The police are going to investigate and they'll interview us, all of us, about what we did or did not see."

Carl rubbed his chin.

"And they're going to search us, Carl."

The men sat quietly for a while, letting the weight of that sink in.

"They'll know we found diamonds up there." Carl looked at Henry, though the darkening night made it harder to see his features.

"Yes. And they might decide we can't keep them for ourselves…"

"So we have to hide them."

"We can't just hide them. They'll know we found a bunch of gems. At best, we can hide some of them, the more valuable ones, and surrender the rest."

"Good point." Carl nodded. "I can see you've been thinking about this."

"Yes. We need a way to keep as many diamonds as we can and get away with them, away from here, away from the police, from everyone."

"What, exactly, do you suggest?"

"Keep the best of the gems in a separate hiding

place. Surrender the less valuable ones when the police force us to."

Carl rubbed a finger across his eyes, thinking. "You know, you can't always tell the difference between diamonds and some of the tiny chips of quartz that are in that sand."

"No." Henry's voice was firm. "The police won't be fooled. They'll take everything we give them to a jeweler."

"No, but they'll believe *we* were fooled. Madison just showed me a handful she thought were diamonds but many of them were just shiny, sharp-edged granules of sand. It's not hard to confuse them. If we mix them."

Henry sat up straight. "I like the way you think, my friend."

"We keep the quartz we find up there tomorrow, along with the real deal, and later we mix a few diamonds with the quartz and sand. Salt the mine, so to speak. That's what we give up, if we have to."

"And we keep the rest of the gems in a separate place," Henry nodded.

"I'm going to start gathering quartz in a bag tomorrow, gather as much of that as we can and have it ready."

"I will, too. And you'll talk to Connor about agreeing to go back up to the pool tomorrow?" Henry asked.

"Already decided to do that."

CHAPTER 46

Brayden watched as brittle stalks of sage crackled in the flames, popping and spitting bits of ash into the air, and he wondered: what had Henry been doing while they were gone? He and Henry had examined Dylan, face down by the stream, still warm but without a pulse. What had Henry been doing before then?

He wasn't squaring up to something. Like the shove from Relic when the grenade was thrown at them, Relic was pushing Brayden away from his position, away from his comfort zone. And the more he stared at the burning flames and thought about it, the more he knew it could be true. Of course he didn't want to consider it. At first, he hadn't even thought it possible. But could it have happened that way?

"Want to talk about it?" Relic folded his hands together.

"Could Henry have killed Dylan?"

"You tell me."

"The more I think about it, the more I realize it's possible."

"Why would he do it?"

"He's hyper competitive and not for some common goal, but for his own status in the company. Dylan was an up-and-coming threat."

"And the diamonds?"

"If Dylan was dead, Henry could gather them up and hope no one else would find them." Brayden lifted a fistful of dirt and hurled it against the ground.

"Last night, you said something about dates and payments? Records with confusing dates, something like that?"

That was it: Brayden's view of the records suddenly popped into his mind and what Relic said about confusing dates made him realize what had bothered him all along – the dates of the payments didn't match the dates of the policies, like they would with payments on commissions. Instead, they matched the dates of the claim approvals, each transfer of money coming within a day or two of the settlement. Damn it all. They were kickbacks on settlements, claims that must be bogus or exaggerated beyond their actual value. And customers would have to have someone in the insurance firm cooperate with that kind of fraud.

"Shit." Brayden pounded his fist into the sand. "I've seen computer records showing, I think, someone taking kickbacks from customers, businesses that bought policies from Henry, or from somebody in our company, but I can't say for sure..."

Relic pulled his flask from his pack and handed it to Brayden, who took a quick swallow and coughed. He held his breath and took another, longer, drink and let the alcohol sear his throat.

"Is there a way to find out? Can you tell if Henry is lying to you?"

"What do you mean?"

"If you confront him, ask him the right questions at the right time, will you know?"

"Damn." Brayden thought about a confrontation with Henry. Could he do it? Murder? Fraud? How could he ask about such things? "I don't think I could handle that."

"Why not? Think it through ahead of time."

"No, you don't get it. Henry's my uncle now, my Aunt Adel's husband, and he got me my job, a great one, at the downtown office."

"Let's take this one piece at a time. Do you want to

keep that job? Is it your career?"

The homemade gin began to pump through Brayden's system, into his bloodstream, loosening his brain. But he knew the right answer: "No. Nothing about that big downtown firm does that for me. Maybe for others, but not for me. I want to be...No, I *am* a writer. I'm a writer, and I want to get up every morning and do something I actually give a shit about."

"See. That settles that. You gotta ditch the job. Now, what about your aunt?"

"Oh." Brayden took another shot of moonshine and thought of Aunt Adel, her buoyant laughter, her watercolor paintings of Lake Michigan in its many moods. He remembered one with long brushes of blue and aqua, splashes of black, a sunset like dripping honey.

"Honestly, I think I would shoot anyone who ever came close to threatening Aunt Adel."

"Then that's your anchor, Brayden. What is the best thing you could do for your aunt, to protect her?"

"From Henry?" He straightened and looked directly at Relic.

"If it came to that, yes."

Brayden stared into the hoodoos. Firelight skittered up, down, and across the stone sentries with disorienting speed, ivory strobes flashing them in and out of sight.

Relic scooted closer. "Do you want to know what I think?"

"Yeah."

"Two things. First, get everyone in your group back on the water and away from the ladder man and his gang of thieves."

"Sure, but how?"

"We don't know what's been going on down there but we need to warn them and get them out of Devil's Tail. Easiest way would be to raft out, but if that won't work, there's a deer trail that runs along the river and they can all use that to get to the next canyon. We won't know exactly how until we get there."

Well, shit. That didn't sound like much of a plan to Brayden. "What else?"

"Second, you're gonna have to come right out and ask Henry if he killed Dylan…"

"What?"

"…and watch his expression when he responds. Don't listen to the words at all. Ignore them. They're his way of distracting you. His reaction, the look on his face, will tell you what you need to know and you can't doubt what you see."

"I can't possibly confront him."

"Why do you say that?"

"I don't...I don't have that kind of courage."

"Bull shit."

"No shit."

"Brayden, listen to me. You've been chased, dehydrated, threatened at gunpoint, and nearly blown to smithereens."

"Yeah?" he chuckled nervously.

"What else could you be afraid of? It takes courage to get through all of that in one piece."

"No, you don't understand. I nearly cancelled this trip altogether. Whitewater rapids? I can barely swim. Desert wilderness? I'm no dare-devil."

"So why didn't you cancel?"

"I was too embarrassed. I didn't want Aunt Adel thinking less of me."

"But you've done all of that now."

"I nearly died in that river. I fell out of the raft and Connor saved me, pulled me back in."

"How does that matter? And what about sticking with me? Finding the airplane wreckage? Braving the heat, the sun, the scorpions? And those thugs who are chasing us?"

Brayden shook his head. "I had no choice. I just had to react to it. I didn't go charging in."

"We all have to react to what comes at us. Swing

the bat at the ball, but don't just drop it and walk away. What's to be afraid of?"

"Embarrassment. Failure. Death. To name a few."

"All of which are inevitable. You can't achieve anything without courage – it's the foundation of all other virtues. Without it, no other virtues are possible, so don't deny it like this. Cultivate it. Look, we've all swerved right when we should have swerved left. But you have to understand something." Relic poked at the fire, red-hot ashes stirred into the sky like fresh stars flaming through the black of space. "We're only passing through this life."

"Yeah. Tell Dylan that."

"Dylan's life is no more tragic or wasted than yours or mine. He, like us, was just passing through, on his way to the next life. Look at it this way: what chance do we have of surviving this world?"

"None."

"Exactly. Our chances of survival are really…" Relic spread his arms wide, "…fat."

Brayden's lips rose in a reluctant grin.

"We're all doomed, you know," Relic lowered his voice in mock despair.

"Doomed…" Brayden's word was tentative.

"Doomed, I tell you," Relic declared.

Brayden had to smile.

"Buddha said, when you realize how perfect everything is, all of it together, you will tilt your head back and laugh at the sky." He spun his finger in the air.

"What?" Who is this Relic guy, really?

"So, you have a choice on your short trip through. You talked about those diamonds earlier. Like they say, you can't take 'em with you. Happiness doesn't depend on whether we have a pile of emeralds," he cupped his hands, "it depends on what we think, and what we do. As travelers, we can drag giant chests full of stuff along with us or we can take just what we need, a carry-on." He pointed to his knapsack and grinned. "All we really 'own' is our power to say yes or no, anyway – the option to do the right thing or not. The rest is just a big junk yard."

Brayden stared into the dust by the fire. "What if you can't tell which thing is the right thing?"

"You do your best. But in this case you know just what you need to do. For yourself. For Dylan. For your aunt. You have to try to find out if Henry is capable of killing someone because if he is, your aunt is in real danger."

"Damn."

"If he's not, then you thank him and move on. But you have to take action. It's the right thing to do."

Just passing through. Relic was right about that,

and it scared the shit out of Brayden. The idea of confronting Henry scared the shit out of him, too, but now he began to wonder why. Does he care anymore what Henry thinks of him? If he's taking the right action, will it matter? Scarier still is the effect on Aunt Adel, if Henry is actually capable of killing another human being. Why would Henry do that?

Of course, he knew the answer: greed. Those damned diamonds, he thought, they bring a person's true nature to the surface, don't they? Then he remembered he had two cigar tins full of diamonds in the "carry-on" luggage next to him and wondered what he should do with them. Henry says you have to take it to make it. What about the question in reverse? What choices will a person make to take it? Ambition is one thing, but the murder, if that's what happened, well, that's just greed, pure and simple.

He fiddled with the lid on his water bottle, still thinking, and after a bit he stood carefully, making sure his legs were solid under him.

"Here, take this." Relic tossed him the fleece blanket.

Brayden wrapped it around his shoulders, its comfort capturing the warmth of his chest. He walked quietly into the night, past the light of the crackling fire. He shuffled around the tough desert sage, over the bumps and dips and stones, feeling his way, following whichever path opened before him and he was soon far from camp and engulfed in the black of the desert sky.

He stopped and thought again about all that had happened and what might lie ahead.

He lifted the blanket so that it covered his ears, and he stared at the western cliffs, a void as solid as rock yet ephemeral as the shadows, a black hole that stole all hope of light – impenetrable, mysterious, and vaporous all at the same time. Above the jagged rim, space itself came to life, filled with thousands of stars, some still, some flickering, sharp, hazy, clusters like hot embers stirred from Relic's fire, floating among the wide trail of our own home galaxy.

He suddenly felt all alone again, like he did the day he hiked on his own toward Devil's Tail, the day he'd nearly died from lack of water, a dry speck of sand on a tiny, spinning, planet, but the loneliness did not scare him tonight. We are creatures of the water and the dust, he thought, made of the very same stuff. We have a relationship with it all, integral and personal, no matter who or where or when we are. When we forget, that's when we feel untethered and lost. That's when we lose perspective. And make our biggest mistakes.

He took a long, slow breath. When we realize how

perfect everything is, we will tilt our head back and laugh at the sky. Score one for Buddha, he chuckled and gawked at the distant stars until their image burned deeply into his mind.

A chill rippled through him and pulled his attention aside. He turned around and watched as their distant fire curved against the strange hoodoos, ripples of light flashing against the smoothness of stone, flames against the auburn heights, as comforting as it was other-worldly. He moved casually back to camp and stood for a bit, mesmerized by the ring of flames at his feet.

"I think you're right about Henry," Brayden spoke into the embers. "Tomorrow, I intend to find the truth."

CHAPTER 47

"Brayden!" Em yelled again, but it seemed hopeless. She and Connor had hurried up the trail early that morning, to try one last time to find Brayden, to no avail. Henry and Carl insisted on tagging along and she could see them, in the periphery, calling for Brayden and searching the ground for shiny objects as they went.

"I don't know what else to do." Connor walked toward her, his eyes on the ground. "We've called and called and seen no sign of him. If he wanted to be found he could have answered, or started a fire maybe, something to let us know he's still alive."

Em heaved the air from her lungs. "Damn."

Henry wandered toward them. Carl stooped close to the ground by the creek, searching through the gravel.

"Time to head back," Connor announced.

"So soon?" Henry glanced back at Carl.

"Yep. The group is waiting for us back at camp. They've been getting ready to leave, so as soon as we get back, we hit the water."

"What?" Henry's mouth drooped open for a moment, unspoken thoughts sending his eyes to the left, then right. "I mean, what about Brayden?"

Em couldn't help wondering if he thought the oars were missing, that they were stranded here. Maybe he couldn't figure out how they were going to go downriver, navigate the rocks and rapids, but he couldn't ask about the missing oars because he wasn't supposed to know. And he had no idea about the spare.

Connor cleared his throat. "We've done all we can to try to find him and we've got to get the rest of the group out of here and call in search and rescue."

"But why can't some of us stay?"

Carl walked up behind them, dropping things into his pocket.

"We're not going to break up the group," Connor glanced at Em. "That's it. We can't risk injury to anyone who might stay."

"What if we insist?" Henry's fingers clenched.

"Look, I can't tie you up and throw you on the boat." Connor crossed his arms. "But we will leave you here."

“That’s not fair!” Carl’s eyes narrowed.

“That’s what we’re doing. It was decided last night. We head out mid-day and bring back help.”

“I’m staying.” Carl looked at Henry, inviting him to agree.

“What about supplies?” Henry asked Connor.

“I’ll leave you supplies for a couple of days but that’s it. If you stay, you’ve separated from the group and we have no more responsibility for you.”

Henry shuffled his feet. “How long will you be gone?”

“Hard to say. We have a lot of water to navigate before we reach the take-out spot. It could be two days before help gets back here.”

“You’re abandoning Brayden.” Carl pointed at Connor.

Henry nodded. “I don’t like it, either. But, you’re not leaving us much choice.” He scratched his head, the tension in his muscles slowly relaxing. “I mean, Carl and I can’t do this alone and we don’t want to be left out here.” He dropped his chin to his chest.

“None of us like this situation,” Em prompted. “But we have to stay together, don’t you think?”

“Look, you can follow Em and me back down or not. Your call.” Connor crossed his arms.

After a moment, Carl turned and stepped away. Henry turned to follow Carl and the two of them spoke in low tones.

Em and Connor shared a glance. She turned and walked toward Henry and Carl, their whispers reaching her as she passed.

"Only a couple in the last four hours..."

"...played out anyways..."

Bastards, she thought. They couldn't care less about Brayden.

She heard Connor following her down the trail and decided not to look back. She didn't give a shit whether Henry or Carl came with them or not. It was time to get the hell out of Devil's Tail.

CHAPTER 48

Brayden rolled onto one elbow and blinked. An early sun shined on the tops of their hoo-doo forest, bleaching their sandstone caps, silver beacons perched atop the rusty chimneys. Shadows smeared away from their crusty bottoms long into the canyon flats.

"You slept well last night." Relic reached into his pack.

"Yeah?"

"Snored like a bear."

Brayden's lips rose. "That moonshine'll do it."

"Sure will." Relic tossed a baggie to him. "Breakfast of champions."

He sat up, pulled his pack next to him, and picked up the baggie.

"I've had some. Finish those, they're all we have left."

Brayden popped a couple of candied peanuts into his mouth, wondering when he'd ever taste bacon and eggs again. "I've got an idea what to do with these boxes of diamonds," he spoke through the mixture of sugar and salt.

"Yeah?"

"I don't think I should walk into camp today with both of these on my back." He pointed.

Relic straightened and smiled. "Smart."

"I want to keep one, in case I need it to bargain with, and I want to hide one. Can you help me do that?"

"Sure."

"You think that's OK?"

"Yeah, I do."

Brayden put the last of the M&M's in his mouth and crunched on them. This could be his last meal in a long time. Or simply, his last meal.

He slowed his chewing.

"We're gonna have to be real careful and real quiet." Relic snapped the top of his pack closed. "Jeb and Ivan could end up ahead of us, on their way back to their camp, or behind us."

"Hmm."

"If they have any more of those hand grenades, all they have to do is toss 'em at us and our ass is grass."

"Hmm."

"I'll keep my sling shot handy, though." He patted his knapsack.

"Against explosives?" Brayden mumbled.

"Why not?"

"Well, are you any good with it?" Brayden pointed.

"I've shot this puppy from hell to breakfast."

Brayden figured that meant Relic had a pretty good aim. He shook his head and stood up then took a long drink of water, emptying his bottle.

"I do need to say something, though," Relic shouldered his pack, grimacing a little at the pain in his ribs.

"Of course."

"You know, I've come to tolerate you pretty well." He grinned. "But I enjoy my privacy out here, and it's best for me to keep, should I say, a low profile."

Brayden put his water bottle away and looked at Relic.

"So, here's the deal. I'm going to go with you as far as the camp, or a ways back from it. If I see a chance to find the ladder man's camp, I'm going to head over there and see what's cooking. I'm here to help you out, but I'm not interested in a whole bunch of introductions, if you know what I mean."

"Of course. Look, Relic, I owe you my life. You

don't owe me anything at all, let alone explanations about staying away from the group."

"Good enough. Just want to be clear about it."

Brayden stood for a moment, thinking about Relic, the rafters, the men who had chased them, and his uncle. And what he would be asking him. He looked out across the grassy flats to the western cliffs, their serrated edge glowing in the rising sun and he remembered the Milky Way, a galaxy full of worlds hidden in the stark light of day but always up there, twirling us into the future, spinning fate.

"We'll refill our water at the creek then scout with the binoculars for signs of the ladder man and his accomplice. We'll take our time and work our way back to the place Dylan died, then back on down to camp."

"And hide one of these cigar boxes."

"Right. I know just the spot."

Brayden nodded and tightened his pack. Ready or not, he figured...

CHAPTER 49

"Shit on a shingle."

"You see something?" Brayden moved closer to Relic. They'd trekked through the hoodoos to a spot Relic knew, buried one of the tins full of diamonds, then hiked to the brook and sat among a scattering of rocks. Relic had searched the canyon with his binoculars in silence, until now.

"Two nuts in a sack. Ladder man and grenade man, making their way to where the dry stream bed from Devils' Tail meets this little creek. I'd guess they're about two miles away."

Brayden strained to see, watching for movement.

"Ladder man has his arm in a sling. That hand's gotta still be sore from the scorpion sting."

"I think I see them, turning away from us."

"Yep. They've come to this stream and are making

their way back down. They must have spent yesterday searching the crash site."

"We can follow them, but this means they'll get to the rafting group before we do."

"Yep."

"Shit."

"You said it." Relic put his binoculars away and stood up. "Like horses, most people don't look back up a trail when they're tired and when they're going back down to food and water. And rest. I think we can get fairly close, we're just going to have to be quiet about it."

"Got it."

"The trail splits into two at the pool below the little waterfall. If they use the north fork, we'll have a chance to get to the rafters first, using the south fork. If they take the south fork, we know they're heading straight for the rafters and in that case, it's not going to be a clean escape."

"Right."

Relic stretched his arms above his head, groaning a bit at the effort.

"Your ribs all right?"

"I think they've been barbequed, but I'll live." He grinned at Brayden then began his way downstream. They wound their way over uneven ground, stepping into the creek bed when the going was easier there. The sun was past mid-morning and the heat was sucking the moisture from Brayden's skin faster than his sweat could rise to the surface. They kept a steady pace until they reached the spot they'd seen the two men turn east to follow the stream. Relic refilled his water bottle and Brayden did the same, washing his hands and arms, filling his hat with water and plopping it on his head to help him cool off.

The brook spread thin at a tangle of rock and they eased their way among them. They stepped past the low rim and kept to the south as the land eased downward and into the jumble of boulders where Brayden and Relic had first encountered each other, running from Jeb and Ivan. Eventually, they came to the edge of the clearing where Dylan had died. They stopped and listened intently, but the air was stifled and still.

Brayden worked his way toward the edge of the low cliff, where the stream trickled to the pool below, and found the trail he'd used to come up with Henry. There, to his left, lay a row of stones in a coffin-shaped pile, pieces of blue tarp peeking eerily from underneath.

Dylan.

The group had buried him here, a few yards from where he died.

Brayden stopped and said a quiet prayer. Maybe it was the heat, or fatigue, or stress, and certainly it was sorrow for Dylan, but he felt like he was floating, watching himself, detached but deeply in the moment, too, seeing his own shoulders shake with a single, deep sob.

"Sorry," Relic put a hand on Brayden's arm.

Tears dried before they could roll off his cheeks.

They turned their heads toward the sharp sounds of splashing water, coming from the wading pool several yards below them.

CHAPTER 50

Relic moved slowly down the switchbacks, stopping occasionally to peer around boulders that lined the trail. Brayden followed as quietly as he could. After several turns in the path, Relic stopped and pointed toward the pool below them. He turned and put his finger to his lips. Brayden found a spot where he could see the water and level ground around it.

"Woo! That's cold!" Jeb shook his head and arms as he walked out of the pond.

Ivan sat in the sand with his boots off, bare feet in the water. "We're almost back to camp."

Jeb wandered in a loose circle, rubbing his face dry.

"What a fucking waste." Ivan wiggled his toes into the sand. "Nothing up that canyon but a ruined old airplane and a bunch of junk."

"We did get to blow up a couple of assholes. We

couldn't even find the bodies they were so deep in the landslide!" Jeb's lips tightened into a gleeful grin. "Dead and buried in one fell swoop!"

"Yeah, well..." Ivan rubbed his neck, a gesture that said he was not so sure the grenade had been a good idea.

"And we found the source of the diamonds, and I found eight more on the trail back down."

"Well, the real payday is yet to come," Ivan jerked his thumb toward the trail, "back at the rafter's camp."

"Yeah." Jeb sat on a low rock by his boots and propped his heels into the sand.

"Bet you never thought you'd find rubies and emeralds on this trip!" Ivan grinned.

"Hell, no. Hey, you never found any Pueblo artifacts, did you?"

"No, I did last year, though, remember? That coffee mug, white with black designs."

"They never drank coffee."

"Not exactly cappuccino, maybe, but cocoa. You know what I mean; a nice mug, all intact, in that first canyon we stopped in."

"Oh, yeah, I forgot."

"But I never dreamed of the haul we've got going now."

They sat quietly for a while, then Ivan pulled his

feet from the water and shook them. He tugged his socks and boots back on and tucked his knees to his chest. Jeb put his socks and boots back on, too, and they both stopped moving.

Brayden thought he heard the sound of tired feet, plodding up the trail.

Jeb and Ivan exchanged a quick glance and stood. Jeb put his holstered 9mm back on his shoulder and they both put their packs back on.

The sound of footsteps grew louder and a man suddenly appeared from around the bend.

"You!" Jeb relaxed his stance.

Henry walked toward them, still breathing hard from the steep trail.

Ivan moved next to Jeb.

"Hey, my group went on down to camp. I hung back and thought I heard someone in the pool so I took a chance I'd find you up here. I can't stay long or they'll miss me." He came closer to them.

"What's going on, Henry?"

"It's all good, Jeb. Most of us came up yesterday and cleaned out this area pretty good." He put his hands on his knees and took a few deep breaths. "I don't think you could find another diamond here or up the creek, way back into the canyon."

Jeb and Ivan looked at each other.

"I wanted you to know we've gathered all we can, and it's quite a haul if you put it all together."

"Good work." Jeb tightened the straps on his pack.

"Yeah, yeah, so when will this happen?"

"As soon as we get back. We'll go to our camp, gather Barc and our gear, then show up at your camp."

"Good 'cause the thing I came back up to tell you is that we took their oars, so they couldn't leave yet, but I found out today they plan to leave anyway, so they must have found the oars, or maybe they have spares, I don't know. They're planning to skedaddle as soon as we're all back at camp, quick as they can." Henry straightened. "So you can't wait. You've got to get there nearly the same time that I do."

"Sneaky bastards." Ivan shook his head.

"But we know now what we have to do." Jeb nodded. "We best get on back as soon as we can."

"Make it look good. Point your gun at me and order me to gather all the stones. I've been keeping track," he pointed to his head "so I know who has diamonds and where they've been keeping most of them."

"Good. We'll see you down there," Ivan nodded.

Henry touched his hand to his hat, an implicit agreement, turned and trotted back down the trail.

Jeb and Ivan moved across the flat area near the pool and onto the northern trail, the one Brayden assumed would take them to their camp, upriver from the rafters.

As the two of them turned a corner and disappeared, Relic and Brayden moved closer to each other.

"Shit," Brayden swore under his breath.

"Why would Henry be in cahoots with these thieves?" Relic asked.

"I don't know, but here's an even better question: why wouldn't he just take off with the rafters when he gets back? If he'd have delayed those guys, like telling them to come get the diamonds tonight, he could have escaped with everyone else, right away."

"And each person in your group would have his or her own small bundle of gems."

"Yes."

"Well, that's your answer. Your uncle wants a cut of whatever these guys take from the group. He must have a deal with them. A deal for a share that will get him thousands of dollars more than he could ever gather up by himself."

"Shit." Brayden put his hand on his forehead and stared down the trail.

"And ladder man and grenade man have all the

firepower. They'll never keep a bargain with Henry or anyone else."

"Shit."

"Unless Henry has a plan to double-cross them, somehow. Let them steal from the group, gather all the diamonds together, then take it back from them. Which is not likely to be a good idea."

"Shit."

"That seems to be our word of the day." Relic's eyes tightened.

CHAPTER 51

"I'm going to follow ladder man and grenade man. See what they're up to," Relic tilted his head toward the trail.

"I feel like I need to get back down to camp and let everyone know I'm OK. Maybe that will spur them to get us all the hell out of here."

"You still have a tin full of diamonds." Relic pointed to Brayden's pack. "Use it wisely, if you need to."

Brayden reached his hand to Relic and they shook. "Thank you for everything."

"You'da done the same."

"Honestly, I might not have before. But now, hell yes." He smiled.

Relic turned and trotted across the open ground to the northern path that led from the pool back down to the river. Wherever the trail ended, he was likely to find Ivan and Jeb, one who'd tried to steal historic artifacts and one who'd tried to blow him up.

He wound his way down the footpath, narrower and less frequently used than the southern trail Brayden would take down to the rafters. Both led to the river, one to a small campsite on the upriver end of the canyon, the other to an open beach and popular area farther downstream.

He continued on for a while then slowed his pace as he rounded a boulder where the path steepened. Something was off. He stopped and knelt behind a desk-sized chunk of sandstone and listened.

Nothing.

No bird song, no rustling grass, no footfalls. Nothing.

Crack!

A broken branch dead ahead. He peered carefully around the large stone. Off trail, above the path and circling back towards it was ladder man, his arm still in a sling. He was only twenty feet below him on the trail.

Grenade man stepped quietly toward the path from the other side.

They'd circled back to try to catch anyone who might be following and Relic had nearly stepped into their trap. He pulled his head back slowly, fully behind the rock and regulated his breathing, listening as the two men came together.

"Nothing."

"I was sure I heard someone behind us."

"You're paranoid, is all."

"Better paranoid than dead."

"Wait. Up there," one of them whispered.

A lone crow flew toward Relic, low and fast, swerving up at the last moment, skimming over the rock and belching its coarse alarm.

"Shit, Jeb, it's just a damned crow."

"I'd like to shoot the thing."

"Come on."

Relic heard their boots hurry across the gravel, sliding in spots down a set of switchbacks. When he could no longer hear them, he rose from behind his rock and silently thanked the crow, now long gone. He moved to a spot where he could watch them and when they disappeared around a bend, he moved quickly down the switchbacks to level ground and continued to follow them at a safer distance. After an hour, he could see the mighty river and where the ground opened up, at the little campsite. He squatted in some tall grass and examined the area with his binoculars, searching the site again and again for any signs of movement.

Two blue rafts were tied to the shore. Nearby was a

narrow, orange and white tent of sorts, the kind used by some for privacy, pitched around their portable toilet. He chuckled at the sight. Must be ladder man's, he thought. But no other tents were pitched and the camp was well cleaned out, the rafts probably all packed for their departure. The men were no longer here, so they must have left for the rafter's site about a mile downriver.

He would have to be quick.

CHAPTER 52

Brayden didn't know what the hell he was going to do once he reached the camp. His best idea, his only idea, was to just walk in and tell everyone he'd been chased by Jeb and Ivan, found the crash site, and came back. It took him two nights because he had to avoid a man with a grenade. He'd tell the story, true to the facts, but leave Relic out of it. But Jeb and Ivan had seen him.

Maybe he was better off telling about Relic but leaving out any details about his new friend, maybe tell people he was just some hiker he met at the crash site and lost track of after that.

But his biggest problem was what to do with Henry. He had to confront him, to find out the truth, but how would he do that? In front of everyone? In private? Would he know for sure whether Henry was lying or not?

His head ached.

He stopped for a rest and long drink of water. The well-worn trail cut across open ground about a mile ahead, a desert pasture of sorts, with patches of grass and sage. Past the gentle slope, the path disappeared again into a jumble of saltbush high as a man's chest. He couldn't see anyone else on the trail, so he resumed a brisk walk down the track.

The mid-day sun heated the back of his neck, so he flipped his collar up. A lone crow crossed in front of him, gliding quietly on blackened wings. Too bad he couldn't take flight like that, scout it all ahead of time. Or ask the crow for a favor. He was soon deeply absorbed in his own thoughts and reached the end of the open area in what seemed like no time at all. He entered a twist in the trail that ducked between the brush, and the rhythm of his boots on dirt lulled him farther into his thoughts as he felt a firmer plan begin to gel in his mind, but as he turned another corner, someone jumped from the bush, grabbing his shoulders, shaking him up and down and his heart nearly stopped.

"Brayden!"

"What?"

"You're alive, you're OK!" Henry stood directly in front of him, squeezing his shoulders. "I'm so happy to see you!"

Brayden stepped back. “Henry?”

“Where have you been, boy?”

Brayden didn’t know what to say.

“Are you hurt?” Henry examined him, head to toe.

“No, no…I’m…”

“Have you seen any strangers along the way?” Henry’s eyes tensed.

“No…” He answered quickly, thinking of Relic, then he remembered Jeb and Ivan. Henry was asking about them.

“Hey,” Henry put his arm around his shoulder. “We have to go now, I mean right now.” He pushed Brayden gently forward and they began to walk side by side. “Camp is just a few yards away and we don’t have much time. There’s something I have to tell you.”

“Yes?” His surprise faded just then and his veins flushed with adrenaline, the fear of confrontation imploding his heart, an empty, wooden shack collapsing to the ground, all his willpower flattened in the dust and he had no idea what to do or say next.

“Carl and I have a handle on this whole deal. Those guys who chased us away?”

Brayden nodded, his blood pressure dipping. He couldn’t possibly confront his uncle.

“They only have one gun. There’s another guy been

watching the camp, but I didn't see a weapon on him. They were going to kill me, but I got them to agree to just steal the diamonds from us all today, then make their escape. But Carl and I have a surprise for them."

His heart clapped a beat. "But they have—"

"No, listen up, Brayden. It's all set to go, right now. We don't have time to talk about this." The trail suddenly opened to a grassy field a few yards deep with flattened patches of ground for pitching tents and, beyond that, a stretch of sandy beach and the floating rafts. Most of the equipment seemed to have been packed into two of the boats, and Connor, Audrey, and the others were gathered around a cooler, seated in camp chairs, eating sandwiches.

"Hey! Everyone!" Henry trotted ahead then turned back to point at Brayden. "Guess who finally showed up!"

CHAPTER 53

Relic hurried to the blue rafts and searched the ground. Two camp chairs and three small tote boxes sat on the edge of the bank, the rafts partially packed with gear. He found crackers and two cans of stew in one of the hard plastic boxes, so he took his pack off and stuffed the food into it. Another box held bags of granola bars, which he slid into side pockets on his pack.

He grinned when he examined the ladder strapped across one of the rafts then jumped into the boat, searching, unclipping dry bags, checking contents, shoving them aside. Beneath the rowing seat was another hard-sided box and he slid it out and open.

"Shit on a shingle."

A row of six rounded, concussion grenades rested on the bottom, each in a thin, foam-rubber cup holder, sliced down the side to expand and accommodate the levers.

He could not suppress a smirk.

His plans suddenly changed. He tossed as much gear as he could from the raft with the ladder into the other one: stove, propane, water, freeze-dried meals, a medical kit, and more. Then he hopped out and ran up the trail to the porta-potty tent. He pulled its stakes from the ground and lifted the thing above his head. Beneath sat the potty itself, something he was not going to touch. But he carried the orange and white tent like a kite, its light fabric fluttering in the breeze, its poles flexing with each step he took. He hopped into the raft and squeezed the willowy frame so that it fit snugly into the bottom, on the side opposite the ladder.

Then he turned, lifted the box of grenades, and stepped carefully back onto shore. He put two grenades toward the bottom of his pack, keeping their make-shift cushions, and placed his sling shot on top, stretching the fabric to close the zipper.

He took one grenade and wrestled with the top, adjusting it to something that might prove even more useful, and hooked it onto his belt.

He left his pack on the ground and returned to the box of grenades. He stepped back onto the raft with the ladder and potty tent and set the container of explosives back on the floor of the boat. Then he removed one grenade, leaving the pin in place, and rested it atop one of the horizontal rungs on the ladder, balancing it, catching it when it rolled off, experimenting with the stability of the rounded weapon on various parts of the aluminum ladder.

The next part would be tricky.

He rested three grenades on separate parts of the ladder, each on top of its lever so that, if it fell, the lever would release if the safety pin had been removed. Of course, after the lever released, the grenade would explode a few seconds later. When he had each of them situated, he scooted to the edge of the raft so he could slide off easily. He slipped the pins nearly all the way out, one at a time, then went back to the first grenade and pulled gently until the pin was fully removed.

While keeping the raft and himself steady, so as not to roll the first grenade off the ladder, he reached for the second grenade and just as he was ready to remove that pin, the first one began to roll off its perch and his heart beat a single heavy stroke, one giant piston pounding down, and he reached, reached, as far as his fingertips could stretch and he caught the grenade just before the lever popped open and ignited its deadly explosion.

He took a breath.

Slowly, he re-balanced the first grenade, turning it to a more stable position. He returned to the second and third ones and removed their safety pins, one at a time. Now, all three were without their pins, balanced, ready to roll into the boat and explode whenever too much motion rocked or jarred the raft.

Relic twisted gently, gently to the outer edge of the raft and lowered himself into the water, holding the craft as steady as he could. When he touched bottom, his motion shifted and the nearest grenade rocked on its lever, backward, forward, backward, well out of his reach this time, the momentum slowing imperceptibly as he slid his hands carefully off the side of the boat, stabilizing it, watching the grenades rise and dip with the subtle movements of the water.

He scrambled up the bank, stepped to the rock where the raft was anchored, and untied it.

The river formed a backwater here, spinning slowly upstream then re-entering the massive flow. One side of the porta-potty tent fluttered in the wind, sailing the boat in one full revolution. He watched as the current began to take its hold, turning the raft upriver for a bit, floating it outward, cautiously, into the edge of the main channel then carrying it lazily down river.

Relic shouldered his pack and ran down the footpath that would take him to Jeb, Ivan, the third man, and the camp of the rafters below. And to the rapids that would bounce the little raft and its cargo of live grenades.

CHAPTER 54

Madison moved into view and slid next to Brayden, touching his fingers, an eager concern in her eyes. "Are you OK? I was so worried about you."

"Yeah..."

She moved closer, almost to a snuggle, and whispered conspiratorially, "Did you find the rest of the diamonds up there?"

"What?" Of course that was what she was after, that was why she was so close and friendly. He pulled his hand back, and her face pinched with resentment.

He turned and stepped away.

"Brayden." Connor strode forward, hand outstretched. "I thought we'd lost you, man."

Em walked toward him, but Claire and Carl kept their distance. George and the others stood from their camp chairs.

"What the hell happened to you?" Connor's smile dimmed a notch. "We've been worried to death."

"It's kind of a…" Brayden noticed movement to his right, a bit upriver, and when he looked his heart slowed, his lungs deflated, and he just stared at Jeb, one arm raised, 9mm pistol in his hand, a chiseled statue rooted to the ground.

He'd tried to warn his uncle, back by the bushes: don't double-cross Ivan and Jeb, just get on the river and get away. He'd tried, but he hadn't done enough.

The others saw where Brayden was staring and followed his gaze. Jeb stood about fifty feet away, not making a sound, not moving an inch.

"The hell?" George, the guide who oared the supply boat, stepped toward Jeb.

Ivan walked into view, a few feet behind and to Jeb's right. Then Barc appeared, thumbs hooked on his belt, watching the group.

Brayden glanced around. Carl crabbed closer to Henry while, Madison and the other guests seemed to slip a step farther away from Jeb.

"You." Jeb spoke to Brayden. "Come closer."

Connor shook his head, a quick command Brayden would ignore. Henry kept his eyes on the three men. Em looked straight at Brayden, her dark eyes wide, and his legs felt heavy as stones, muscles sore, hunger long ago turned to exhaustion, but he shuffled across the hard-packed dirt.

"Closer."

Brayden took another stride toward Jeb, a stronger one this time, determined to face the man who'd nearly killed him and Relic, the explosion still vivid in his mind. He stared into the man's pale eyes, small and glassy, then Jeb slid a pair of mirrored sunglasses onto his face, the effect cold and unnerving. Then Jeb took a short step forward and, faster than Brayden could see, the pistol had lowered to shoulder level and the man took another quick step and everything slowed, though he was sure it was moving fast, and the muzzle grew in his sight, the black hole at the center expanding exponentially, a tunnel from which the bullet would blast at any moment, and Brayden focused on standing still, knowing he'd be dead soon, willing himself not to blink or flinch so at least he could die with some dignity. And then Jeb squared his hips, a shooting stance. Brayden expected to die momentarily, and he heard the hammer click back and took one final breath before the squeeze, the flare, the end of his quick journey through this world.

"Hey, mister!" Henry lifted his arms and walked toward Jeb. "We have something you want, something you're going to want to see."

Jeb stopped.

Brayden couldn't breathe.

"Diamonds. Bags and bags of them" Henry spoke like he was out of breath, his words a little jagged.

Jeb's lips curled slowly, a man appreciating a humorous remark. He turned casually toward Henry, like he'd known all along that he was going to come forward.

"What's your name?"

"Henry."

"Diamonds?"

"Diamonds."

"Show my friend." He nodded toward Ivan and his aim rose just a bit above Brayden's head.

Henry walked to Ivan and held open a narrow cloth bag. Ivan peered inside and nodded at Jeb.

"Gather all the gems into that bag," Jeb commanded, "from everyone here." He swung the gun in a low arc across the group.

Henry nodded rapidly and ran to Carl, who emptied something from his pockets and dropped them into the bag. He went to Madison, who seemed rigid in shock. She shook her head at first, but Henry insisted until, finally, she emptied her pockets as well.

The rest of the group gave up their jewels without

resistance or delay until the bag seemed filled to the brim.

Henry turned back toward Ivan but spoke to Jeb. "We give you these jewels and we all go free, right? No shooting, no harm, no foul. Right?"

"Sure." Jeb's voice was flat, emotionless. He pointed the pistol into the air, resting his elbow on his side. He turned toward Ivan and took two steps in his direction.

Brayden finally took a deep breath.

Henry handed the bag to Ivan, who removed his shirt, slid it gingerly over his swollen palm, and spread it onto the ground. Using his good hand, he began to pour the diamonds onto the cloth.

"Hey, we've done our part," Henry pleaded.

"That's all of it." Carl took a step away from Jeb and Ivan.

Ivan chuckled with glee as he spread the gems around but, as he emptied the last of it onto the shirt, his smile faded and his face tightened. He stirred the pile again and again, anger reddening his cheeks.

"Half of this is nothing but sand!" He threw some of it down in disgust.

"Hey, some sand got in the bag is all." Carl took another step back. "It's all there, everything we collected."

Jeb lowered his pistol and fired it at Carl's knees.

CHAPTER 55

The deputy rowed closer to shore and called out: "Anyone here?"

One blue raft was tied to some bushes, but the camp was mostly cleared and packed away. Well, he thought, whoever is here can't be far.

He pushed his raft against the grassy bank and hopped out. He walked it a ways from the other raft, close to a sapling, where he tied it up. He climbed the bank to an area recently flattened with tents. From there, one trail wound its way uphill, into the canyon. Another followed the river downstream.

He touched his pistol, an old habit, making sure it was in his holster, then thought to get his satellite phone and first aid kit. He hopped back to the boat, fell part way in, grabbed them and a small daypack, and stumbled back up the bank. He tucked the items into the pack and slung one strap over his shoulder.

He made his way along the trail, roughly parallel with the river, moving upslope, then down, until he'd gone nearly a half mile.

Pow!

He recognized the sound right away, a pistol, maybe a 9mm, very close, and ran down the path as fast as he could.

CHAPTER 56

Gunfire echoed against the high sandstone, bouncing across the canyon, and Brayden watched as Carl fell, slow motion it seemed, to the ground and Claire ran forward, clutching at him as he dropped, but Carl was so suddenly limp it seemed his bones had melted.

Brayden couldn't move.

"Now…" Jeb spoke as the sound of the gunshot faded. "Henry. It seems you have some more diamonds for us, right?"

"Yes, yes." Henry had slid to his knees, his voice a mere tremor, no longer the negotiator confident in his success.

"Then let's get on with it." Jeb aimed the pistol at Henry and, though his gaze was focused there, Brayden sensed a blue raft in his periphery, a strange looking orange tent, of sorts, perched within it and the unusual sight drew some small part of his attention.

"What the hell?" Barc shouted, pointing at their floating porta-potty tent when a deep blast hit the air, ejecting the tent like a rocket, splitting the raft and a silver-colored ladder in two, firing a stream of water high into the air, a Yellowstone geyser, steam and spray and debris scattering through the sky, pieces of it splashing into the river, rolling onto the beach.

They all were stunned, transfixed by what they'd seen, their ears ringing, their skin tingling, the blast absolutely deafening.

"Who the hell did that?" Jeb roared.

Barc ran toward the rafters, glaring at each of them in turn. "Answer us!"

Jeb took aim at Henry again.

"I've got the rest of the diamonds, Jeb, they're on the boat, I'll get them right away," Henry said, a snag in his bravado, a rush to finish his sentence.

Jeb cocked the pistol.

Suddenly, Jeb's head crimped at a terrible angle, hard against his shoulder, then bounced back, but his knees dropped him downward and he pulled the trigger, another blast echoing through the canyon as he collapsed into the dust.

Brayden turned to see Relic, slingshot in hand,

poised to shoot it again. He pivoted and fired at Ivan, who squealed in pain and dropped to the ground, his uninjured hand holding the side of his head.

Barc pulled a small pistol, a short-barreled gun Brayden hadn't seen before, and aimed it into the group of rafters, and just as Brayden wondered where Relic was, why he hadn't used his slingshot again, he realized he stood directly between Relic and Barc, blocking his line of sight.

Em stepped in front of Madison and the others, a human shield, her eyes and lips tight with worry.

"Hey!" Relic's voice was urgent.

Brayden spun back toward Relic.

"Dud," he mouthed silently to Brayden then tossed a grenade straight at him, its pin removed.

Brayden caught it with both hands, twisted toward Barc, and pitched it in a high arc. "Catch!"

Barc's mouth opened wide and round as a billiard ball, his eyes intent on the incoming grenade, and his fingers stretched instantly outward, his gun falling toward the ground, his arms and neck and face shaking with palsied fervor and he turned and flung himself hard to the ground and rolled away, arms over his face.

Everyone waited a beat for the explosion that never came.

Em ran to the pistol and lifted it with two fingers, like something hot and smelly she'd rather not touch, and carried it away from Barc, who still had his head on the sand, legs now tucked in a fetal position. Audrey stepped forward, took the pistol from Em, and stood between Barc and Ivan, aiming the gun at one, then the other, and back again.

Em turned and trotted toward Henry.

Brayden ran to Jeb, who was still lying on the ground. He slid the nylon belt from his pants, wound it around Jeb's left wrist and pulled it tight. Just then, Jeb seemed to wake, his muscles twitching, his head turning from side to side. Brayden reached for Jeb's right wrist and tugged it toward the middle of Jeb's back, winding the belt once around it. Suddenly, Jeb curled at the waist, slipping his right wrist away, away, nearly free of the belt. Brayden dropped his full weight onto Jeb's back, forcing a breath of air from the man's lungs, tightening his grip, but still he felt Jeb's wrist slipping away and just when he thought he'd lost, he yanked the belt on Jeb's left wrist high between his shoulder blades, higher, higher, until Jeb cried out in pain, relinquishing, finally, and Brayden re-wrapped the belt around both wrists and knotted it again, again, and again.

Pow!

A man stepped toward them from the path, pistol raised in the air, and as he moved toward Brayden, Relic tucked his slingshot away and turned his back to the man.

"Sheriff here! Deputy Dawson! Everyone hold their ground!"

Now Brayden noticed the tan shirt, pleated, shoulder patch with a silver star, and felt his stomach slowly unclench. Relic walked backwards toward the officer.

"Everyone halt!"

Relic stopped and raised his hands, his back still toward the deputy.

Audrey slowly lowered Barc's pistol. "I'm one of the guides. These men shot at us!"

Dawson stared at her intently then nodded, a signal that she should keep her guard.

"Help!" It was Em's voice and when Brayden looked, he saw Henry laid out on the ground, Em keeping his head up, blood soaking his shirt.

The deputy holstered his pistol, stumbled past Relic, and ran to Henry.

Brayden glanced toward Relic and saw him give a brisk salute, a prompt goodbye. Brayden returned the gesture as Relic turned and trotted back up the path toward the campsite used by Jeb and his crew.

Brayden stood and hurried to see his uncle.

CHAPTER 57

"Everyone, get back!" The deputy waved his arms, broad breaststrokes through the air, and kneeled next to Henry. "You!" he pointed at Connor. "Get a tourniquet on the other guy!"

Connor ran toward Carl.

Brayden moved past Madison, George, and the rest of the group and slid to the ground near Em, who held Henry's head. "I'm his nephew," he said to the deputy, who nodded.

Deputy Dawson packed a gray, powdery substance on Henry's side. Brayden assumed it was to staunch the blood.

"Take this Percocet, it'll dull the pain." The deputy rolled a pill into the palm of his hand then placed it on Henry's tongue. "I'm trained as an EMT." he glanced at Em, who helped Henry take a drink of water.

"Is he shot?" Brayden heard the urgency in his own voice.

"Yeah, but I don't know if it hit anything vital. I've done what I can to stop up the wound and gave him a painkiller. Does anyone here have any medical or nursing skills?"

"I do," Em brushed the hair from her face.

"Good. Stay with him. I'll check the other guy and call for helicopter rescue." Dawson stood and walked away.

Brayden looked at her, his question implicit.

"Wilderness medicine."

Brayden sat cross-legged on the ground and felt for his uncle's wrist. "Henry, can you talk to me?"

Henry's cheeks seemed gray and pasty, his eyes squeezed partially shut. He shifted to a more comfortable position, grimaced, then gasped for air.

"Hold still," Em scolded.

Henry seemed to catch his breath and relaxed a little. He blinked and looked around. "What happened?"

"You got shot," Brayden said. "By one of those thieves. We think it missed anything vital, but the deputy is calling for a helicopter to get you to a hospital."

Em nodded. "It hit you on your side, not very deep. It looks like you'll be fine." The look she gave Brayden said she was not so sure.

"Wait, a sheriff? What happened here?" Henry asked.

"Yeah. We're OK, but the gunman shot Carl." Brayden said.

"Oh, god, the sound of the gun..."

"Right. And the gunman shot you, too, but he shot wide, I guess."

"Oh, no." Henry's eyes were fully alert now, tinged with worry. "Carl's shot?"

"Yes."

"It was our idea, our plan. To pretend to give them the diamonds but put sand on the bottom of the bag, keep most of the gems for ourselves."

"The guy with the injured hand, he poured it all out onto his shirt, on the ground, and found out what you'd done," Brayden said. It was a ruse like the one he and Relic had used, not to keep gems for themselves, but to garner some help from the scorpions and get away. Those thieves were not going to be fooled, especially not twice in a row.

Henry stared into the distance.

Dylan was dead, Brayden thought, and his uncle had something to do with that, too. He could hear people shuffling in the distance, talking in low tones, the deputy asking questions, giving directions, but it was all just background noise, a buzz that hummed in his head. He remembered his talk with Relic, his niggling fears that Henry was stealing insurance money and had murdered Dylan, his alarm at what it all might mean for his Aunt Adel and he decided there was no other time, no better time, than to ask the questions.

His stomach felt like molten lava.

"Henry." He squeezed his uncle's arm, and the reality of it swept through him again, but he kept Aunt Adel in his mind, and Relic, and this time his courage held.

Henry looked at Brayden, his eyes alert.

"I have to ask you something serious. The day before we left on this trip, I went to your office to check some of the employment records, for the reports. But I found a bunch of records, claims, and money transfers to an account in Montreal. The payment dates match the dates the claims were paid, not when the policies were sold."

Henry blinked.

Em squinted, her expression puzzled.

"Those were payoffs to you, weren't they? Your cut of a bunch of fraudulent claims."

Henry tensed and looked away. "Dylan and I were just adjusting our commissions, to what they should have been each year."

"Dylan, too?"

"But those records were my proof that he was taking more than me, short-changing me on our partnership."

Damn it. He leaned closer to Henry. "Now I have to ask you something even more important."

"Yeah?" Henry's tone was sarcastic then he shifted and winced.

Em's eyes showed a hint of fear.

"Did you kill Dylan, up above the pool, above the little waterfall?"

Henry's face went slack and he stared at his shoes, as if they'd become a center of fascination. His silence stretched into time, a solemn paste in the air, thickening everything, a great and suppressing muck, and his eyes cooled, a pair of dull, gray bullets and Brayden knew he'd found his answer.

After a moment, his uncle cleared his throat. "I didn't mean to do it…"

Brayden narrowed his eyes.

"Really, I didn't." He shook his head, glancing at Em. "I went up there to find Dylan. He was at that little creek then he stood up." Henry turned directly to Brayden. "He said he'd found diamonds and I laughed at him. But he held out his hand and, sure enough, he had a fist full of them and then he laughed at me, said he'd found them and they would all be his, his claim had been staked under 'common law,' he said. I told him he was full of shit, there's no such thing, and he shoved me and said he'd have lead sales position, too, by the end of the year, it was my time to 'crawl away,' he said, and retire. I told him I'd found proof that he was cheating me, taking kickbacks on his own, no longer splitting them like we'd agreed, and he shoved me hard again. This time I took a swing at him, hit his chin and he went backwards and down, onto a piece of driftwood..." The words tumbled out of his mouth in a rush and he had to take a breath. "That's the honest to god truth. I knelt down next to him, expecting to hit him again, but he wasn't moving, so I rolled him onto his side and saw some blood on his forehead. I wiped it away, to see if I could see the wound but the cut wasn't very deep and I couldn't figure out why he was unconscious. I kept trying to wake him up, but he was totally limp, so I kept trying and trying and that's when you showed up," he pointed at Brayden, "and we couldn't get a pulse and I freaked out. I didn't tell you and we didn't have time anyway 'cause just then, that's when Jeb and the other guy showed up with a gun and chased us away."

Brayden watched as his uncle's expression shifted

from worry to fear to confusion and then to a plea for understanding he'd never seen in the man before, and Brayden decided then and there that he believed him.

"How did you know the gunman's name? How did you know Jeb?"

Henry didn't hesitate. "I ran into those boulders by the trail, still above the pool where everyone else was. I lost you, didn't know where you'd gone, but the one named Jeb followed me. He found me, Brayden, and was going to kill me then and there. He already knew about the diamonds. Like I tried to tell you earlier, I tried to make a deal with him: I'd keep the rafters here, in this canyon, gathering gems for another day or so and then Jeb's guys would rob us and escape, clean away. I wanted Jeb to let me live, and you, too…"

Something about his uncle's words bothered him. "And what else?"

"Well," Henry winced and pressed against his wound. "I also bargained for three percent of their take."

"Shit."

"Hey," he spoke quickly again, "I figured he wasn't going to go for any of that, that he'd expect me to double-cross them, and that's just what Carl and I tried to do, but I would have said anything to keep him from shooting me then and there, anyone would have done that Brayden, anyone in my position."

Brayden looked at Em, her brown eyes wide with surprise. "And your double-cross went sour."

"Yes." Henry hung his head. "Carl was going nuts for those gems, you could see it on his face, and I decided to make an ally of him, see if we could keep most of the diamonds for ourselves."

"Just the two of you."

"Well…"

"You have to take it to make it?"

Henry looked away.

"I get it." He stared at the canyon rim behind Henry and Em, following its jagged line across the sky. Wealth without work leads to injustice and violence, he thought.

"Aunt Adel is going to have to know all of this, when we get back."

Henry looked up again, his face transformed, and his glare could have cut glass, but Brayden no longer cared what Henry thought or did. He was done with him, hell and away forever.

CHAPTER 58

Henry's expression gradually softened and his mind seemed dulled and distant. Brayden heard boots plodding behind him.

"How's our patient?" Deputy Dawson asked Em.

"I think that pain pill is kicking in."

"I don't see more bleeding."

"Yes, that's stopped, and I believe he's comfortable."

"Can you lay him down? Connor! Get me something soft for Henry's head, will you?"

Brayden watched as Connor brought a fleece jacket to Dawson and rolled it into a make-shift pillow. Em lowered Henry's head as his eyes closed. "He needs a blanket," she said to Connor, who trotted off to the rafts to get one.

Em and Brayden stood, watching Henry doze.

Someone groaned several yards away and they

moved quickly to see who it was. Carl sat with his legs flat on the ground, bent at the waist, his hands propping up his back. Claire knelt next to him, her hand on his arm.

"You're all right, Carl."

He seemed disoriented, a teenager wakened too early in the morning, his hair ruffled, his wire-rimmed glasses a little bent. He looked up at Brayden and Em, then over to Claire.

"The bullet grazed your leg, just below the knee." She pointed. "I've wrapped it with my T-shirt and it's not bleeding anymore."

Carl put his left hand on his face and drew it downward, stretching his eyelid, holding his cheek for a moment, then let his palm slide down to his thigh. "Oh, man. I thought I was going to lose my leg."

"Yeah," Claire said softly. "You passed out for a while."

He glanced about the camp. "The diamonds. We still have the diamonds, right?"

"Right." Claire pulled her hand away and stood. "And yes, Carl, I'm OK."

"Good." His head seemed to be clearing. "Henry. Is Henry all right?"

"He's been shot." Brayden stepped closer. "But we stopped the bleeding and we think he'll be OK."

"The diamonds?" Carl's eyes betrayed a craving.

"A deputy sheriff is here now. I'm sure the police will want all the diamonds back," Brayden said.

"I'm sure they will." Carl grinned, some kind of silent conspiracy keeping his spirits up.

Em turned to Claire. "How are you holding up?"

But Claire ignored Em and Brayden and stared into the distant mesa for what seemed like a moment of darkness. Then her eyes tightened on Carl, her face reddened, her hands cramped into fists, and something seemed to burst inside her, something festering, and in a voice deeper and cooler than Brayden had heard from her before, she said: "Carl, I will not marry you, not now, not ever. I have nothing more for you and you have nothing more for me. We are going our separate ways." She slid a zirconium ring from her finger and tossed it into Carl's lap.

Claire shook her fingers loose, extending her hands and arms from her body and into the air, a preacher reaching for the heavens, and she seemed to rip her gaze from Carl, turning it toward the high cliffs across the river, smiling contentedly.

CHAPTER 59

Relic trotted for a while, until his ribs began to ache, then slowed to a walk on his way back to the thieves' camp. He'd seen Jeb fire his pistol, but the marble-sized rock in his sling shot had dropped that nutcase to the ground. The arrival of the sheriff's deputy was wholly unexpected. Relic had kept his back to the man, lest he get a good look, and hoped the confusion would keep him out of focus until he could depart.

He rounded the last corner in the footpath and found the second raft just where he'd left it. Downstream from that was another raft tied to a sapling: the deputy's boat.

He would not disturb it.

He made a quick search of the campsite for anything that might be useful but found nothing else he really needed. The blue raft was filled with gear, three tents and sleeping bags, a small propane stove, pots and pans, drinking water and a variety of stews, soups, tortillas, and spices. He'd hit the jackpot. He put his own pack into the raft.

He untied the boat, stepped inside, and positioned himself in the rowing seat. Three deep strokes took him into the main current and then he really put his back into it, rowing as fast as he could, slipping across the wide river toward the distant shore until he thought the rafter's camp would soon come into view. Then he pulled the oars out of the water and stuffed them inside the raft. He slid to the bottom, shoving bags and tents out of the way. He lay as deeply as he could, well below the inflated sides, and waited as a pair of puffy clouds spun gently above him.

Muted voices and clunks and clangs reached his ears, and he knew he was floating past the rafting group and the deputy sheriff. He listened for any change in the clatter, any shift in the babble that might show he'd been seen.

A short set of rapids raised and lowered the raft as he drifted, rocking it, splashing along the sides, and when the camp sounds began to recede, he lifted his head for a quick view.

No one along the shore was waving or shouting or

moving their rafts into the water to catch him. It seemed he was going by unnoticed.

He dipped below sight again and waited several more minutes. When he sat up, he'd passed the tall, auburn cliffs that marked the southern end of Devil's Tail. No one else was on the river. He positioned himself again in the rowing seat, pulled out the oars, and began a casual spin of the boat.

Five miles down, the river bent to the right, and he recognized the little canyon. He rowed out of the current and into shallow water near a stand of willow saplings, flushing a white-faced ibis into flight. He rowed as far as he could up the winding drainage until the boat scraped the sandy bottom where the water petered out. No passing boaters could see him here, and the drainage made for an easy trail to pack out the gear. He had two locations in mind for caches, one west and north of here, and one to the south. He would make several trips, take one five-gallon jug of water and canned food part way to the first site, then repeat the process for the second. Before long, he could push the raft into the main current and let it float wherever it wanted, likely to be retrieved by campers. It would not be found anywhere near the little canyon he'd pulled into. Later, he'd take each of the food and gear caches the rest of the way to sites he'd scouted long ago, shallow caves away from any beaten paths, protected from unwanted guests. And he'd take a grenade to each camp, too. Just in case.

CHAPTER 60

It took Brayden a moment to process what Claire had just said to Carl, but when he did, he shared a knowing glance with Em. Two relationships had ended on this trip, but maybe there was room for new ones now. They stepped away from the former couple.

"The chopper will be here in about thirty minutes." The deputy walked toward them, displaying his satellite phone. "It's a small one, so it can just take Henry and Carl, first trip. It will come back and take the thieves on a second trip. And Connor's outfitter will load replacement oars on the chopper, so you can all raft on down to the take-out spot."

"Thank you." Brayden offered his hand to the deputy, who seemed surprised but smiled and shook it warmly.

Jeb and Ivan sat in the dust with their backs to each

other, hands tied or cuffed, George and Audrey keeping a close watch over them. George held his left hand awkwardly, like it had been hurt. Barc lay in the grass on his own, hands tied to his feet.

"I need statements from everyone," Dawson said to Brayden. "But your group will be heading out soon on one of the rafts, so you should join them."

"OK."

"One quick thing, though. Some folks said there was a man standing behind the man with the gun, but other folks didn't see him. I'm trying to figure out if there was a fourth man among the thieves or not. Do you know?"

Em looked at Brayden. "Not me."

Brayden shrugged.

"Oh, well, I guess we'll figure it out eventually." Dawson scratched under his hat and wandered off.

"Let's sit over there." Em pointed to a spot on the beach and they walked in that direction.

Just then, the sliver of a small blue raft appeared on the river, a good distance away from their camp, floating empty on the rippling current. Brayden stopped and stared and, for just a second, he thought he'd seen a head pop up from below the sides of the boat, then disappear, and he knew exactly who it was. And he knew who'd been responsible for the exploding tent.

No one else seemed to notice the blue slice rising in and out of sight behind the waves, disappearing forever around the corner.

Em had found a place on the edge of the beach and pulled her knees to her chest. He walked over to her.

"Did you know all that stuff your uncle said?"

"No. I suspected worse, actually."

Her dark eyes stared up at him.

"I thought maybe he'd murdered Dylan. Now, I think it really wasn't intentional. Still, the insurance fraud, the killing, the greed; it's all a lot to think about…"

"No kidding."

"Weird, too, to think he was trying to protect me."

"He just said that to manipulate you."

Brayden sat next to her. "Yeah, I know."

"Connor said it would take a day and a half to get to the take-out spot."

"That's fine by me. Might even help me process some of this, before we get grilled by the police, when we get back."

"I still can't believe what Henry said." Em shook her head.

"Yeah. Thing with him is, he'll revise that story over time, so keep what he said clearly in mind. Don't let him bend it later on."

"You don't like your uncle very much."

"True. But I love my aunt, and she's going to hear about all of it."

"Henry's responsible for Dylan." She twisted a blade of grass between her fingers.

"Yeah."

They sat in silence for a while, watching the river flow steadily past, eddies spinning near the shore, small waves chopping over rapids farther out. He scanned the base of the cliff on the other side of the river, searching the cracks and ledges, roving upward over the smooth red rock all the way to the rim. A falcon soared above the edge, a casual miracle of flight, and Brayden had a sudden urge to journal it all, to purge the fraud, the killings, the chase, to celebrate the hoodoos, the rugged gorges, the gin-brewing recluse.

Em leaned her arms on her knees. "What's your next step, after we get back?"

"Well, I know a couple of things."

Em looked at him.

"I'll quit the job in Chicago. I need a whole new start."

"Makes sense."

"So, I'll need another job, but I'm thinking I'll

come right back here, after I wrap things up in Illinois."

"Need work here?"

"Yeah, you got any leads?"

"Well, my non-profit group plans to focus on climate change and how it's affecting the canyons here, all up and down the Colorado and Green rivers. You said you're a writer?"

"Yeah."

"What kind of writing do you like?"

"Any kind, for work."

"Right. And for fun?"

"I've been thinking about a journal and maybe some poetry."

"That seems fitting for a place like this." Em looked around. "It's hard to capture in mere words, even in poetry."

"Capture's the wrong idea. You don't capture a place like this. You develop a relationship with it."

Em turned toward him quickly and laughed, a burst of joy at such a simple thing he'd said, and the effect was contagious. Tiny lines lit the corners of her burnished eyes, as welcome and warming as old friends, and he smiled back at her.

"Well, we might have a place for you in our group, you know, some work for you."

"Really?"

"Well, I'm not the boss, so it's not up to me, but I can put in a good word." Her brow rose.

"Could the job include another trip with you on the river?"

Her cheeks may have flushed a bit, but he wasn't entirely sure.

"Yeah. We don't have much money, but some. We're trying to raise funds for a study of the climate change here. We need a real investigation, a scientific one, to measure the effects. With that, we think we can get some grass roots action, force Congress to help protect these places."

Sunlight glistened on the muscled river, its broad shoulders sweating, tendons bunching over boulders and bedrock.

Brayden straightened his back, shifting the old cigar tin in his knapsack.

"Non-profit, you say?"

Her nose crinkled a bit. "Yes?"

"How would a guy make a donation?"

"I thought you needed a job."

"I do. But I prefer to share the rest."

CHAPTER 61

Deputy Dawson stood near Henry, who lay resting on the ground. Dawson was within quick reach of Jeb, Ivan, and a man they called Barc, all of them seated in the dirt, hog-tied, disarmed, and dejected. He'd talked to Sheriff Coyle directly on the satellite phone, arranging helicopter transport for Henry and Carl. He was glad he'd remembered to get Connor's outfitter to send oars back with the chopper, if they could; getting these rafters out of the canyon and back to the safety of the take-out spot was also a priority. There, other county deputies and federal officers would meet and interview them and, most likely, collect the jewels they had gathered in Devil's Tail. They were evidence, after all.

None of his prisoners were saying what had happened, but that wasn't going to matter much. It was obvious they'd tried to rob the rafters of the gems and that

Jeb had shot Henry and Barc had shot Carl. There were plenty of witnesses.

But what about the missing man? The one with a ponytail, who kept his back to him during the initial take-down? No one seemed to know about him, and when Connor did his head count, everyone was accounted for, even the rafter whose body remained above the little waterfall. Dawson scratched behind his ear. Could the missing man have been the one he was searching for? There was certainly enough water higher in the canyon to keep a still for cooking illegal moonshine.

He thought about the brief moment he'd seen the man, trying to recall details. Was he tall, short, thin, heavy? Not much had really registered; the shooting, the adrenaline, all of it happening so fast. But Dawson was pretty sure the man's hair was dark and long, tied in a ponytail. It was, wasn't it?

This was going to bug the hell out of him.

Well, he thought, he'd stay here until the prisoners were gone and the rafters floated away. When he was alone again, he'd work his way up-canyon toward the body, take some pictures and notes, keep an eye out for the desert bigfoot and any signs of a gin-brewing kitchen. He hadn't found any ghosts on this trip but he'd stumbled into the crime of the century. Well, for these parts anyway, and maybe he'd get a commendation after all. But that did not mean he was done searching for the moonshining hermit, no, indeed. He couldn't prove a thing but he knew he'd been here, he knew it in his bones.

CHAPTER 62

"Hey." Audrey stepped in front of Em and Brayden, interrupting them. "I heard what Henry said to you. Just wanted to say 'sorry' and if I can do anything to help, please let me know."

"Thanks, Audrey. You heard all of that?"

"Yeah."

The three of them watched as Deputy Dawson went from Connor to Madison to George, small notepad in hand, interviewing each of them. A helicopter would arrive soon enough, Brayden thought, bringing more deputies and investigators and interrogations and searches.

He still felt the weight of the cigar tin full of diamonds in his pack. Would there be a reward? What if their owners were dead or out of business? Would he be able to keep the gems long enough to donate them to

Em's non-profit? How could he legally convert them into cash? If he was going to figure this out, he needed to hide them, at least for a little while.

"Excuse me." He touched Em's shoulder as he stood.

"Sure."

He made his way downstream, past the rafts to a spot where the beach petered out then he climbed onto the shelf above. From there, he looked right and left, searching for privacy and a landmark he could remember later on.

Scattered voices rose and fell in waves as he stumbled past a knoll and into a low spot in the canyon, a place where he could no longer see the boats, tents, or anyone at all. Twenty yards away, in the middle of the natural depression, rested a blood-red chunk of sandstone the size of a pickup truck. He moved to the other side of the rock, where the sounds from camp evaporated. Four book-sized blocks of stone rested on the bottom of the large rock. He moved them aside and put his pack on the ground.

He removed the cap from his water bottle and used it to dig into the sandy soil at the base of the big stone, and when he'd finally gotten five or six inches deep, he stopped and inspected the hole. He listened carefully. He stood and walked around the rock, examining all he could as he went, taking his time. No one was around. He returned to the back side of the stone and placed the tin of diamonds into the dirt.

He filled the soil on top of the tin, patted it down, and slid the chunks of stone on top, hiding the fresh dig. He poured water over the lid of his bottle, wiping it clean, then he swept the ground nearby with his hands, further hiding any sign of disturbance. He sat back and examined his work.

He tried to do a rough calculation. How many gems were in the tin? If every gem were worth a thousand dollars, on average, the tins a hundred square inches, the jewels in the ground in front of him were worth about two and a half million, both tins together, maybe four. "Whoa," he exhaled slowly.

When he and Relic were at their second camp, the one in the sandstone hoodoos, he hadn't been sure what to do with the boxes of gems. Now, he resolved to leave forever the tin that he and Relic had hidden up there. Relic didn't have a greedy bone in his body, but if he ever really needed them, he could get them, use them to meet his need.

As for the diamonds buried in front of him, he'd want to forget them, too, for now. "There," he brushed his hands together, feeling the finality of it, knowing he need no longer worry about the cigar tins, each safe in its own secret storage. Buried treasures. One tin would soon be used to help protect these desert canyons – after the official investigations had been completed.

He stuffed the water bottle into his pack, moving his steno pad out of the way. He'd scribbled a word or two but hadn't really written anything yet. In fact, he hadn't written anything in a very long while, everything all plugged up like a water balloon straining to burst, and now it would. Now it was going to flow like the broad Colorado and he would be stirring, sweating, brewing it into something that might make some sense.

The sound of spinning blades echoed against the sandstone and he knew it must be the rescue helicopter, hurrying toward them, its distinctive *whop whop whop whop* rising to a crescendo.

He'd best get back to the others.

CHAPTER 63

Brayden loped back to the sandy beach, where all three rafts had been packed and passengers boarded, except for George, who stood nearby, and Em, who held the anchor rope for George's raft. Audrey rowed in long, deep pulls, taking her, Madison, Claire, and three others into the slow, brown current. Connor and his passengers, minus Henry and Brayden, sat waiting in their boat.

George approached him, resting one arm inside the other. "I've pulled a muscle in my left hand somehow, so I've asked Em to ride with me in the supply boat, but I could use another to help."

"To row?" Brayden hadn't ever thought about doing such a thing.

"Yeah, wanna go first?"

He looked at George, then Em, whose quick smile seemed to betray some slight conspiracy. Had she encouraged this?

"I'll walk you through it. No big rapids for several miles, and we can stop to scout them before we run them."

He heard himself say "Sure," his voice sounding a little foreign. Courage, he thought, the foundation for all other virtues.

Em nodded her approval and motioned for Brayden to get into the rower's seat. He hopped onto the side of the raft and scrambled past the gear. A wooden bench with a waterproof cushion bridged the raft, the oars on either side, so he sat there and grabbed the handles.

"Let Em push us out and get in, then lift the oars and we'll do a lesson for you both." George settled into the boat.

Em shoved hard against the raft, the bottom scratching over the sand until all of it was afloat, then jumped on.

Brayden pushed on the oar handles, leveraging the paddles upward and held them there. The current swung them gently away from the shore. Deputy Dawson gave them a quick wave and he could see Henry being helped into the helicopter.

Leaving Devil's Tail seemed strange, and Brayden felt oddly sentimental, but he had no time to wallow in it. The main current yanked the raft like a chain on a log and turned them quickly downstream. Soon, they would be past the canyon, all of it behind them.

"Now, keep the oars back towards you, that's right, now dip them into the water ahead of you, then push forward." George pointed. "Remember that they move on a fulcrum, so motion is sometimes backwards. Push down to lift them out of the water. Pull them back to you before you drop them back in, then push forward to move forward."

He fumbled with the heavy oars, pulling when he meant to be pushing, lifting when he meant to be dropping, but eventually he understood the mechanics and managed to spin them forward.

They heard the sound of helicopter blades *whomping* through the canyon, the echoes dissolving away, Henry and Carl heading to a hospital.

"Row just one oar and see how that turns you, then do that with the opposite one. Just get a feel for how it moves, and don't worry about where you are in the river right now. Let's just wander for a while."

Brayden did his best to follow George's instructions, and he began to get the feel of it, rowing a bit here and there, keeping their raft headed downriver, glancing at Audrey's boat ahead of them and the canyon rim above. He overcompensated for a rightward drift and they circled all the way around, waving to Connor's raft forty yards upriver from them. George and Em shifted about, nestling between dry bags full of tents and sleeping bags, George propping his injured hand on the side of the raft.

Soon they were watching the cliffs roll past, a small herd of mountain sheep gathered by the riverbank, and the humble excitement of rowing a whitewater raft amazed him with its simplicity. He never expected to wrestle a pair of whitewater oars in his hands, riding down the middle of the Colorado River. Really, how fat were the chances of that?

He remembered the wading pool, his friend the desert recluse, and his homemade gin. He remembered the tin of diamonds he'd buried and his hike in the upper reaches of Devil's Tail, its whip-saw curve, its pointed edge. The sight of those two fliers high in the gorge, their skulls and bones scattered across the ground, made a new impression on him just now as he realized that he too, had become a jewel thief of sorts, brothers-in-arms with the daring aviators of Devil's Tail. He never expected to find the nerve of a thief, the grit of a bush pilot, or the sudden bond he felt with it all, and he raised his face to the sky and laughed.

AUTHOR'S NOTE & ACKNOWLEDGEMENTS

Thank you for reading *Diamonds of Devil's Tail* – I really hope you enjoyed it! As an author, I depend heavily on book reviews and referrals. So if you think others might enjoy the novel, too, please leave a quick review on Amazon and on any other internet site you use for selecting books to read. *The moment it takes to leave a quick book rating makes a lasting difference for the author!*

I want to acknowledge my parents, family, colleagues, and many accomplices. Though too many to recognize all of them, the names of a few have been used in the story – place names, company names, or such – as a quick "shout out" to those fine people, who deserve a lot more.

Thanks to all who understand their kinship with the planet and those who work in the service of their ideals.

Thanks also to all my family and friends who have shared canoes and rafts with me over the decades: Gina, Sarah, Adam, Sarajean, Nate, Doug, Dave, Ron, Jeff, Bridger, and many others. The rivers of this nation deserve and depend on our respect and preservation. Their waters are sacred.

I thank Jim Dempsey, at Novel Gazing, for his careful attention to detail and insightful suggestions. Thanks also to Dad, Gina, and Sarah for their solid editing suggestions and to Gina for letting me disappear for hours and days at a time while working on this effort. And I thank Nate again for the incredible map art at the front of the book.

Thanks to Daniel Thiede for the fabulous cover art and text layout!

Though there are too many names to list them all here, my many good friends and colleagues with the Northern Arapaho Tribe deserve special recognition.

And, finally, I thank the many people who have inspired the characters in this work.

EXCERPT FROM

DESERT GUARDIAN

The roar of whitewater drowned out all other sounds of life, even Ethan's own breathing. He watched with a sense of awe as Anya powered her boat to the left, deftly guiding it as she watched the rapids on their right.

Ethan followed her move, paddling to line up with the left shore, then rowing toward it.

In mere moments, a huge rock appeared on their right, the river bellowing over it like a jet engine. Water reared high above the rock, spraying whitecaps into the air, plunging into a crater of water below, swirling and rising and collapsing on itself as it went. He could feel the waves rocking his raft even several yards away. As quickly as the sound had engulfed him, it started to fade.

"Ethan!" Anya yelled across, her voice a mere reminder among the sound of throbbing rapids to look up, pay attention.

He saw her rowing toward the right shore. Quickly, he spun the raft so his back was to the same shore and began to row.

The current was much faster here than in the

stretch of flat water he'd gotten used to. He could hear and sense the rapids directly in front of him. He dipped the oars and pulled mightily with mediocre results. He forced himself to row faster and harder, desperate to avoid the coming whitewater.

The sound of the first rapid he'd passed was nothing compared to the vibration and roar of the waves ahead. All he could do was keep rowing, putting his legs into it, straining his back against the oars.

Without warning, the front of his raft dipped sideways into a trough, nearly tossing him out of the boat. His upriver oar swung through thin air, angled out of the water. He leveled out for a moment, bracing himself. Then the raft buckled inward as it crashed into a wave ten feet above his head. His hands slipped from the oars and found brief purchase on the center frame. The river pounded him like a waterfall. He lost all sense of direction as the raft spun high on the cresting water, spray blasting his skin like shotgun pellets.

The raft slid sideways across the downriver slope of the high wave. He was weightless for a moment as it fell toward another trough and then, at the bottom, the raft buckled again, tossing him clear of the boat like a piece of cork.

He had time for only half a breath before the

cold water sucked him under, spinning him down through the roiling currents. He struggled for a second, flailing his arms and legs, then stopped. As water pressure began to hurt his ears, he knew he was too deep to swim up, that he'd use his air too quickly if he tried to fight the current. Let the life jacket do its job, he thought, if it can. He forced himself to relax, to conserve his energy, to let the river take him where it would. To do that, he had to surrender - fully, unconditionally – to the power of the water, the flow of rain, snowmelt, and desert springs all merged into one gargantuan muscle of river tearing through bedrock itself, carving grand canyons out of solid stone. What could anyone do against that?

His arms and legs tingled painfully then went numb - from the cold or lack of oxygen he could not tell. His mind flashed to Relic's water bottle. Water, the one thing he could not live without in this harsh and beautiful desert; the one thing that would now kill him. He would never take water for granted again.

Though his eyes were closed, stars and spears of light flashed across them. He spun more slowly than before but disorientation had seized control. Was he right side up? Rising? Sinking?

His chest burned like molten magma, cooking

and crackling, dying for a simple gasp of air to release the flame. His muscles moved involuntarily to expel his breath but he forced them back. He knew he had to breathe, and soon, even if it meant sucking his lungs full of water, but he rallied back against the thought, squeezing it out, willing himself to never breathe again. When his throat convulsed, the world became a void.

EXCERPT FROM

RAPTOR CANYON

The tent became a dome of light, then began to smolder and burst into flame near the back, near the kitchen stove.

"Hey, we just cleaned the grill back there," Relic said, making Wyatt laugh.

The fire spread slowly, casting a halo of light across the camp. Security guards hollered, workers yelled their curses and questions, and everyone rushed to see what the commotion was all about.

"Is she really crazy enough to do that?" Wyatt asked.

"Yep," Relic nodded.

"Well, shee-it," Wyatt did his best imitation of Faye.

Relic smiled. "Don't let her hear you or she'll knock your block off."

"No doubt."

"Would you see what you can do to slow down that backhoe up ahead of us and anything else with a lock and key? Then work your way north, swing back toward the staircase and we can meet up there."

Wyatt nodded.

"Keep a close look out. They'll be searching as soon as the mess [kitchen tent] is under control."

"What's your next move?" Wyatt asked.

Relic jerked his thumb toward the portable toilets.

"Really?" Wyatt said.

Relic turned and faded into the dark. Wyatt heard footfalls, someone moving quickly toward him. After a moment, he recognized her shape bobbing along. She tossed something and he heard it clacking into the bed of a pickup. She nearly ran into him.

"Hey." He put his hands out toward her.

"Hey," she said, slowing, but only a bit. "Here." She tossed a stick of dynamite to him, the fuse sparkling lit.

"Shit!"

"Throw it!" she shouted as she ran past. "Now!"

Wyatt stared at the tube in his hand. The fuse sputtered and spat and shortened with every second, time compressed with the tightness of his breath, the glowing fuse moving forward immutably until something like a spinning clutch popped in his chest and muscle movement became possible again. He reached his arm back and threw it as far and as fast as he could, then he spun and ran to the side of another truck and turned back to look.

The pickup Faye had tossed something into rose into the air with a smack that washed away all other sound, then fell back to the ground with a nasty twist as pieces of sheet metal dropped from the sky.

"Holy..."

Wyatt's stick of dynamite exploded somewhere beyond another truck, lighting something on fire, sending a second sonic boom through his skull, making him jump in his tracks. He stared at the blaze as it settled into a steady burn and looked the direction Faye had run.

A third, fourth, and fifth explosion erupted in quick succession in the row of portable toilets and Wyatt knew it was Relic's work. Where was Relic's peaceful resistance now? Lord, he hoped no one was in those toilets. Then, he thought, what a mess of shit, and he giggled and smacked his hands together.

Oh, my god, was it possible to have so much fun? He never expected stopping Lord Winnieship from stealing this canyon to feel so damn good.

He stared at the fire he'd started and tried to think. He wanted to follow Faye but there was no telling what other mayhem she had in mind, and he did not want to walk into an exploding outhouse. He tried to regulate his breathing, with only a little luck. He circled away from the path Faye had taken, giving her a wide berth, moving to the outer edge of the parked vehicles.

Wyatt turned and trotted toward a lone backhoe, maybe sixty yards away. Though the electric lights of the compound were out, the kitchen and dining room blaze cast a sallow glow on the tops of the other tents and equipment. The upper arm of the yellow backhoe was lit like a candle.

His shins scraped across brittle sage and he slowed to a walk. He'd lost his own toothpicks, so that trick [of jamming the locks] would not work with the heavy equipment. After Faye's dynamite, toothpicks seemed pretty pathetic anyway. Maybe there was a set of keys kept in the ignition that he could toss away. Or maybe he could flatten its tires or pull wires from under the dash to disable the beast. He turned to watch the bobbing of flashlights all around the burning mess tent a quarter of a mile away. The voices of men rose and fell in a rhythm that was almost musical, like an offbeat composition.

He stopped at the base of the backhoe and stared up at the top, where the boom and dipper attached. He circled the machine to the open cabin and peered inside.

"Stop and turn around." The voice was deep and familiar.

Wyatt turned and raised his hands. Even in the semi-dark, Lynch's muscled bulk identified him immediately. He held a pistol aimed at Wyatt's chest.

"You!" Lynch said. "You sonofabitch."

Wyatt saw the left hook a milli-second before it struck his jaw, wrenching his head away and toward the ground. He stumbled to the side. A blow to his stomach struck like a rocket and his chest ached, all the veins in his body shut down by a sonic boom. Slivers of light flashed through his eyes, closed tight against the assault. He sensed himself floating to the earth, his muscles turned to liquid. He was out before he hit the dirt.

EXCERPT FROM

WINGS OVER GHOST CREEK

Owen thought his heart had completely halted, and it had, for just a second, and then it began a pounding, deep and strained, pumping blood through his temple in spurts then galloping quickly, flushing his cheeks.

Holy flying eff.

He sucked a shallow breath of air, pulled his gaze from the dead arm, and looked back the way he'd come. From this perspective, the arm was well-hidden on the backside of the long pile of dirt, tucked close to the low rock face and well out of view from the hangar and the tents beyond. Last night's heavy storm had flushed loose soil from the canyon slopes and probably from the body, too. He tried not to look back at the fragile hand, but he couldn't help himself. Skin shriveled against the tiny bones, stiff leather holding the assembly of joints together, keeping the fingers pointed in confusing, haphazard directions, their owner not sure which way to go. Red nail polish added a cheap party flare, a celebration completely out of place.

Holy eff. Hold it together, he told himself, get back to camp and pretend he'd never seen it. Tell Thomas. No one else. Someone here could have killed this girl, must have killed her. Why? What had happened here?

He turned his eyes to his feet and shuffled across the ground, moving to the edge of the pile of dirt. He peered around the mound and saw the edge of the hangar and the back of the tents. No one seemed to be around, so he hustled away from the dirt, across the hard-packed surface, and into the hangar. He went to the yellow plane again and leaned on the right strut, his breath still shallow and labored.

Owen looked beyond the hangar to the field outside and the Cessna waiting for them. Where was Thomas?

"Did you get that cold drink?"

Panic charged through his brain, a devil's hot wire crackling from one ear to the other. His head jerked toward the front of the plane and he clamped his hands tightly on the strut. Everett's question was smooth but – was there an undertone in his voice?

Owen managed to force a breath.

"No..." he patted the wing support, glanced at Everett, then spoke to the plane itself, too nervous to look at the man again. Squeezing the strut helped him to focus. "I got sidetracked by this old Aeronca. What year is it, do you know?"

"1946, I'm told."

"Oh."

"Are you a pilot?" Everett moved out of the sunlight and into the shade of the hangar. Owen knew the man could see him better now.

"No, no, I'm not. Tried to take some lessons, but…" He struggled to keep his thoughts on the aircraft, away from what he'd discovered. "Just look at this panel, the instrument panel," he pointed. "Not hardly any instruments here, though. It's all metal, too, like the dashboards on old cars." He kept his eyes on the cockpit, still reluctant to look directly at Everett.

"Yeah, I've looked it over myself." Everett's voice seemed more normal now, more conversational. "The owner has a friend who came out here a couple of days ago. He's restoring the old bird, but I don't know how far he's gotten. The fabric looks like a stiff breeze would pull it off." He ran his hand across the edge of the wing opposite Owen. "You wouldn't catch me flying in this death trap." Everett wandered away from the plane, plucked a long blade of grass from the ground and began to twist it absentmindedly.

"Yeah, the cloth on this one needs completely replaced." Owen tried to sound like an authority on the subject and felt his nerves calm a little as he spoke. He ducked under the wing and walked into the sunlight.

"Seen my boss?"

"I think he's about done," Everett pointed toward the tents along Ghost Creek. Thomas and Angela were walking slowly back toward the Cessna. Angela was explaining something, Thomas nodding.

"Well, it was nice meeting you." Everett moved quickly toward Owen and offered his hand, his smile show-room friendly, his shake cold and curt.

"Yes. Nice meeting you, too." Owen made eye contact briefly and turned back toward the Cessna. "Better get going."

He strode toward the rented Park Service plane, muscle memory moving his legs, thoughts flowing back to that tortured hand, its ragged movement in the breeze. He tried to be nonchalant about getting the hell out of there. Angela and Thomas came closer to the Cessna.

"Got what we need?" Owen asked Thomas.

Thomas looked up. "Yep. Thanks for the tour and good luck to you," he said to Angela. He shook hands with her and Everett and turned back to the plane.

Owen did not wait to be told to climb in. He adjusted his seatbelt, put the headset on, and waited. Thomas did the same.

How was he going to tell Thomas about the dead girl's arm? When should he tell him? Angela and Everett positioned themselves to one side and in front of the Cessna. They could see any conversation between him and Thomas, so he stayed quiet.

Thomas spent a moment examining the air map and checking the instruments. Out of the corner of his eye, Owen saw the man with the red hat, Luke, run up to Everett and whisper urgently in his ear. Everett glared at the plane, then gave some sort of order to Luke, who ran out of view. Did they know he'd found the girl's body?

"Clear prop!" Thomas pumped the throttle and turned the key, the engine spitting to life. Owen sat back in his seat, eyes straight ahead, and listened to the engine as Thomas adjusted the fuel mixture and checked the magnetos, turning first one off, then the other, then both back on for flight, Owen wishing he would hurry the hell up. Thomas finally pushed the throttle forward and the engine roared, the Cessna shuddered, and they began to roll down the dirt strip, vibrating, bouncing, jarring over small ruts until suddenly, liftoff, and the ride became smooth and even, the engine solid and throaty, clear air ahead of them, and Owen finally took a deep breath.

Thomas made a gentle turn to their left, flying back toward the creek, the dig site, and the old hangar, circling to gain altitude needed to fly over the plateau above the camp. They rose steadily as they went, Owen thinking how to explain what he'd found, hoping he'd done the right thing by waiting until they were in the air, bound for home base.

They leveled out about two miles past the Quonset hut, aiming for the broad Colorado River as they continued to climb beyond the canyon. A ribbon of dust rose to their right, a truck in motion along the road, soon to be well behind them. Ghost Creek faded from view as they neared the level of the plateau. They could see the bronze river beyond as it wound its way southward, on toward the Grand Canyon, on to the Gulf of California. Owen rubbed his hands on his pants and readied himself.

"Thomas," he spoke into the microphone on his headset.

"Yes?"

"I've got something to tell you, something I discovered down there while you were with the archeologist..."

"Yes?" Thomas checked his GPS and adjusted his heading.

Just then, a hollow thump jarred Thomas forward and he pushed the yoke in, then tugged and released it as he slumped back in his seat. Owen grabbed the yoke and his eyes swelled wide and he stared at Thomas' slackened face and began to scream his name, bobbing the plane's nose up, down, up, when another hollow thump jarred them and oil sprayed into the air and onto the right side of the windshield and he heard the motor cough, and cough again, and felt the Cessna lose its power, dropping in the air, descending toward the ground and he screamed again.

A moonshining hermit.
A campus bookworm.
A midnight murder.

Ethan's world turns upside-down when he slips off the edge of red-rock cliffs into a world of twisting ravines and coveted artifacts. Saved by a mysterious desert recluse named Relic, Ethan must join a whitewater rafting group and make his way back to civilization. But someone in the gorge is killing to protect their illegal dig for ancient treasures... When Anya, the lead whitewater guide, is attacked, he must divert the killer into the dark canyon night, but his most deadly pursuer is not who he thinks... Ethan struggles to save his new friends, face his own mortality, and unravel the chilling murders. But when they flee the secluded canyon, a lethal hunter is hot on their trail…

Can an unlikely duo and a whitewater crew save themselves and an ancient Aztec battlefield from deadly looters?

Readers' Favorite says:

Desert Guardian is an "engaging action… mystery"

The novel features "tough, credible characters"

Readers' Favorite Five Star Review

Grand Master Adventure Writer's Finalist Award

Buy now from a bookstore near you or amazon.com

ALSO AVAILABLE FROM

A. W. BALDWIN

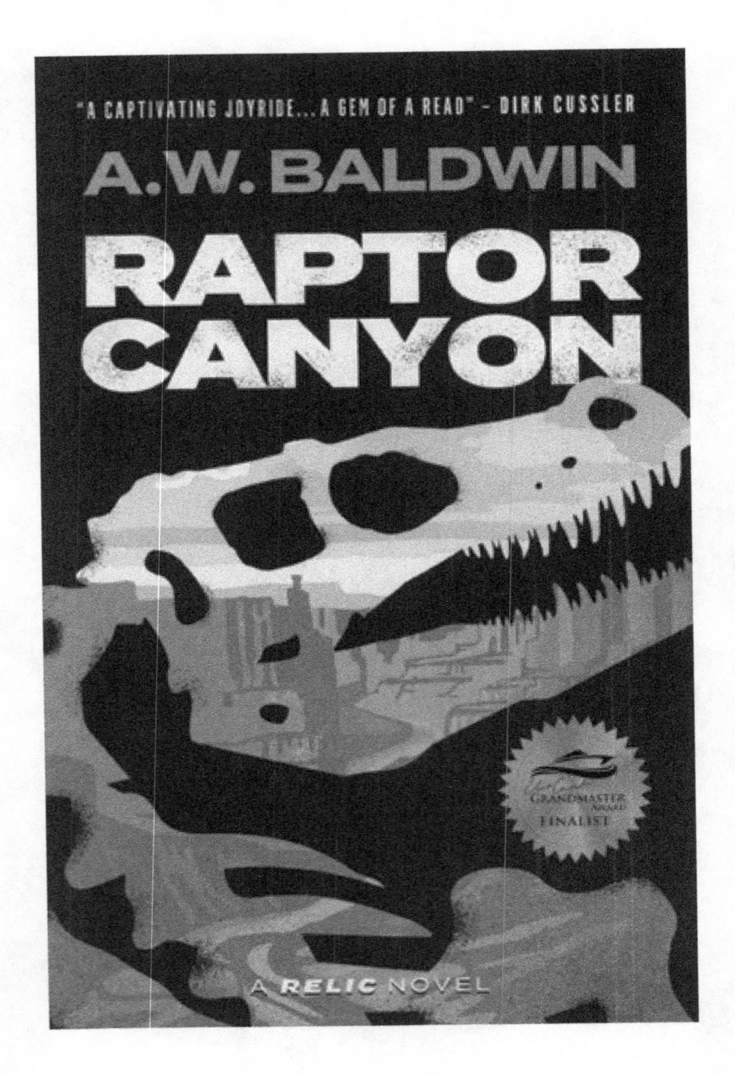

A moonshining hermit.
A big-city lawyer.
A $35million con job.

An impromptu murder leads a hermit named Relic to an unlikely set of dinosaur petroglyphs and to swindlers using the unique rock art to turn the canyon into a high-end tourist trap. Attorney Wyatt and his boss travel to the site to approve the next phase of financing, but his boss is not what he seems... When a treacherous security chief tries to kill Relic, Wyatt is caught in the deadly chase. The mismatched pair must tolerate each other while fleeing through white-water rapids, remote gorges, and hidden caverns. Relic devises a plan to save the treasured canyon, but Wyatt must come to terms with the cost to his career if he fights his powerful boss... A college student with secret ties to the site, Faye joins the kitchen crew so she can spy on the enigmatic project. When she hears Relic's desperate plan, she has a decision to make...

Armed with a full box of toothpicks (and a little dynamite), can the unlikely trio monkey-wrench the corrupt land deal and recast the fate of Raptor Canyon?

"A gem of a read..."

–Dirk Cussler, #1 *New York Times* best-selling author

"[You'll be] holding your heart and your breath at the same time..."

- Peter Greene, award winning author of
The Adventures of Jonathan Moore series

"A hoot of an adventure novel..."

- Reader's Favorite, Five Star Review

Grand Master Adventure Writer's Finalist Award

Screencraft Cinematic Book Contest Semi-finalist

Buy now from a bookstore near you or amazon.com

ALSO AVAILABLE FROM

A. W. BALDWIN

"A BEAUTIFULLY WRITTEN THRILLER" - READERS' FAVORITE

A.W. BALDWIN

WINGS OVER GHOST CREEK

ADVENTURE WRITERS AWARD WINNING AUTHOR

A RELIC SERIES NOVEL

A moonshining hermit.
A reluctant pilot.
A $5million plunder.

Owen discovers a murdered corpse at a college-run archeological dig in the Utah outback but when he and a park service pilot try to reach the sheriff for help, their plane is shot from the sky. Owen must ditch the aircraft in the Colorado River, where he is saved by a gin-brewing recluse named Relic. The offbeat pair flee from the sniper and circle back to warn the students but not everyone there is who they seem... The two must trek through rugged canyon country, unravel a baffling mystery, and foil a remarkable form of thievery. Suzy, a student at the dig, helps spearhead their escape but the unique team of crooks has a surprise for them...

Can they uncover the truth and escape an archeology field class that hides assassins and dealers in black-market treasure?

"A beautifully written thriller."

-Readers' Favorite Five Star Review

"[A] humorous, fun, and well-plotted adventure. Baldwin is a master storyteller…"

-Landon Beach, Bestselling Author of *The Sail*

"Baldwin delivers another gripping Relic tale with trademark wit and deft expression. This is adventure with philosophy that keeps you nodding your head long after you've put the book down."

– Jacob P. Avila, *Cave Diver*, Grand Master Adventure Writers Award Winner

Wings offers "…action-packed adventure and nerve-racking suspense, with a touch of romance and humor mixed in." Baldwin has a "gift for capturing the reader's attention at the beginning and keeping them spellbound"

– Onlinebookclub.org review

Grand Master Adventure Writer's Finalist Award

Buy now from a bookstore near you or amazon.com

CPSIA information can be obtained
at www.ICGtesting.com
Printed in the USA
FSHW012302060321
79253FS